# I'M AN ALIEN

AND I WANT TO GO HOME

# I'M AN
# ALIEN

AND I WANT TO GO HOME

## Jo Franklin

ILLUSTRATED BY
## Marty Kelley

HOUGHTON MIFFLIN HARCOURT

BOSTON NEW YORK

Text copyright © 2014 by Jo Franklin
Illustrations copyright © 2015 by Marty Kelley

First published in Germany in 2014 by Coppenrath Verlag.

www.hmhco.com

The text was set in Adobe Caslon Pro.
Book design by Lisa Vega

The Library of Congress has cataloged the hardcover edition as follows:
Franklin, Jo.
I'm an alien and I want to go home / Jo Franklin ; illustrated by Marty Kelley.
pages cm
Summary: Daniel has only two friends, is unusually tall, is picked on by teachers, and
does not look like anyone else in his family, so when he learns his mom saved a newspaper
clipping about a meteor that landed nearby on his birthday, he embraces his pretend alien
heritage and launches a mission with his two friends to return to his home planet.
[1. Humorous stories. 2. Honesty—Fiction.] I. Kelley, Marty, illustrator. II. Title. III.
Title: I am an alien and I want to go home.
PZ7.1.F753Im 2015
[Fic]—dc23
2015006822

ISBN: 978-0-544-44295-5 hardcover
ISBN: 978-0-544-93824-3 paperback

Manufactured in the United States of America
DOC 10 9 8 7 6 5 4 3 2 1
4500661539

For Eleanor and Cedric

# CONTENTS

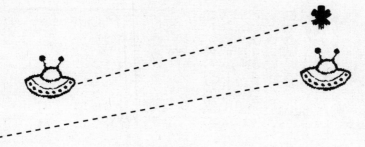

# 1

## My Family — The Kendals

Mom and Dad claim they met on a nudist beach in the tropics somewhere. These days they are only nudists in the shower. I am also a nudist in the shower, but I wear clothes at all other times.

My incredibly annoying older sister, Jessie, has a Random Mood Generator. Her favorite tracks are Psycho, Bossy, and Mega Mean.

When Mom lost her wedding ring, she located it using a metal detector. It was in the body of my baby brother, Timmy. She had to dig through all his dirty diapers until she found it. She still wears it. Gross.

We live at 26 Beechwood Road. Dad thinks our address is boring, so he named our house and stuck a sign on the front. He thinks calling a house Konnichiwa ("hello" in Japanese) is cool. He is wrong.

No one in my family knows my name. They call me Bean, short for Beanpole. I happen to know that my name is Daniel Kendal.

I have *nothing* in common with my family.

# The Big Fat Family Secret

I like to eat breakfast on my own before going to school. It's safer and quieter that way. Every day, I eat four single-serving boxes of Mega Flakes, which I stack like two double-decker buses parked next to each other on the table. I need the calories to feed my growing legs, which are very long and very hungry.

Today I was still eating when Jessie came in to annoy me.

"What is it with you and those freaky long legs, Beanpole?" Jessie said, waving her hair straightener around like a pair of manic chopsticks.

"There's nothing wrong with my legs." I was unarmed. I grabbed my cereal boxes and built a wall across the kitchen table.

"They're weird and I don't want them anywhere near me." Jessie snapped her straightener at my feet.

3

I pulled my legs back to my side of the table. No way was I letting her grab me with those superheated jaws. I was already the tallest kid on the planet—I didn't need to be covered with stinky burnt hair as well.

"I don't even know what you're doing living in this house," she said.

"I'm your brother."

"Really?" Jessie pushed the cereal boxes off the table and got right in my face.

I had a clear view up her nose. I wasn't sure how Jessie got that hair straightener up there without

4

burning her nostrils, but the hair in her nose was definitely straight.

"Wanna know the family secret?" she said. "The one about you?"

"There are no secrets in this family," I said. This is one of Mom's favorite sayings.

"No secrets?" Jessie said in her sarcastic voice. "Really?"

She was right and Mom was wrong. There were lots of secrets in our family, and I knew some of them.

1. Mom said she'd given up chocolate, but I'd found a giant almond Hershey bar behind the microwave, and the bar kept getting smaller.

2. Timmy knows three bad words. I taught them to him myself.

3. Jessie had a puff on a cigarette at Uncle Jimmy's fortieth birthday party and then she was sick. (Serves her right.)

4. When Mom thought Dad was cutting Mrs. Jenkins's hedge, he was actually fixing Miss Duffy's car. Dad calls Miss Duffy Carol. Mom calls her Killer Heels.

5. I'll be getting a new bike for Christmas. I wasn't supposed to know, but I saw the catalog with a page ripped out. I hoped Mom would order the right bike. She likes pink, but I hate it.

These were my top-five family secrets. I didn't think the big fat family secret Jessie was referring to was my new bike.

Jessie's Random Mood Generator was stuck on Mega Mean. "You aren't really my brother," she growled.

An icy chill crept up my back and wrapped itself around my neck.

"You're an alien, abandoned on Earth by your alien parents." She snapped her straightener at me.

"Dad didn't want you." Snap.

"I didn't want you." Snap.

"But Mom felt sorry for you. And now we're stuck with you." She whacked her stupid straightener at my head as she got up to leave. "Why don't you take your alien legs and go back where you came from? And you can take Serena Blake with you. She loves aliens."

"Serena Blake?" I said. "Who's that?"

"A nutjob in my class. See ya later, alien boy." Jessie threw a crust of toast at me and stormed out.

What did she mean? Aliens didn't exist. Except in movies, and those aliens had tentacles, crazy black eyeballs, or telescopic necks.

I wasn't like that. I was normal. Well, not exactly normal, but I was convinced I was one hundred percent human.

So what did Jessie mean? She said I wasn't really her brother.

A rock of doom smashed me in the stomach.

Was she telling me I was adopted?

# 3

# The Trouble with Photographs

I was still wondering who I was when Timmy charged in and pointed at me.

"Bean," he said. "Bean bad."

"Thanks, buddy, I'm beginning to realize that." I slumped on the chair, the rock of doom so heavy, I couldn't stand.

"Bean!" Timmy bashed my knees with his fists. I held his pudgy hands and looked at him closely. Then I thought about the other members of my family and what they looked like.

| | TIMMY | JESSIE | MOM | DAD | ME |
|---|---|---|---|---|---|
| EYES | Baby blue | Evil blue | Normal blue | Bloodshot | Mud brown |
| HAIR | Blond with cereal | Blond with hair gunk | Blond with help from hairdresser | Missing | Brown |
| HEIGHT | Toddler | Teen plus heels | Normal plus heels sometimes | Shorter than Mom | Taller than everyone else in my family, my school, and my neighborhood |

My conclusion: I didn't have a single strand of DNA in common with any of my so-called family.

When Mom and Dad came into the kitchen, all I could do was stare. How come I'd never noticed it before? I looked nothing like them.

"Jessie gone to school, Bean?" Mom said as she strapped Timmy into his highchair.

"Duplo!" Timmy shouted.

"She told me I'm not her brother," I said.

"Oh!" Mom and Dad said at exactly the same time, as if they were telepathic. It's perfectly normal for best

9

friends to be telepathic, but it was totally weird between a mom and a dad, particularly when they were being telepathic about me. I thought their reason for freaking out at exactly the same moment was that the truth about my misfit DNA was no longer a secret.

"I'll speak to Jessie later," Dad said. "Remind her that we're supposed to be nice to each other."

"Duplo!" Timmy banged his fists down on the tray of his highchair.

"Jessie can't be nice," I said. "Why did she say that? I want to know the truth."

"Don't take any notice of Jessie." Dad picked up the toaster and turned it upside down, as though the bread was stuck inside. I guess Dad was studying the guts of the toaster as a way of avoiding my question. His bread was still sitting on his plate.

"Where did I come from, Mom?" I said.

"It started with a little egg and a little seed, but I haven't got time for this now, Bean." Mom grabbed a cereal bowl and slammed it on the table. Her ears had turned bright red, as if she was embarrassed. She knew I knew all the sex ed stuff, so I figured she was embarrassed because she was hiding the secret about me being adopted.

"That's not what I'm talking about." I kicked the chair. "I mean *me!*"

"Can we talk about this later?" Mom didn't even look up. "Timmy, it's breakfast time. No Duplo bricks at the table."

"Duplo!" Timmy shouted.

"Cereal!" she shouted back.

Timmy prefers toast. But Mom won't give it to him, not since the time I taught him to play toast Frisbee and a stray piece stuck to her backside. It could have saved her a trip to the sandwich shop at lunchtime, but a dog found it before she did and nearly ripped her skirt off.

Toast Frisbee is now forbidden in this house.

"How did I come into this family?" I said.

Dad cleared his throat and stared out the window.

"Open wide, Timmy," Mom said as she tried to push the spoon into Timmy's mouth.

"Any more butter?" Dad asked.

"In the fridge," Mom said.

I felt exactly like that piece of Frisbee toast. Lonely and stuck somewhere I didn't belong.

Dad was too busy avoiding the little egg/little seed talk to listen to me.

Mom was too busy looking after Timmy.

My parents didn't want to speak to me, their maybe-adopted son. I needed hard evidence. Then they'd have to tell me the truth.

I grabbed my backpack and pretended I was leaving the house. But I sneaked into the family room instead. The photo albums were on the bottom shelf of the bookcase.

Every year on New Year's Eve, Mom goes through all the photos she has taken that year and picks out the best ones for the album.

I pulled out the album for the year I was born and flicked through the pages. My birthday is in April, so I expected to find myself a quarter of the way through the album.

Photos I found:

- Jessie in a Snow White outfit, trampling over seven dwarfs.
- Jessie ripping a teddy bear's arms off. Mom had written underneath, *She hasn't changed.*
- Jessie at the beach with no clothes on.

I turned the page quick. Jessie was only four in the

photo and I hadn't even been born, but I didn't need to see her training to be a nudist.

After that, the pages were completely blank.

Mom's photo album for the year I was supposed to have been born was empty. There were no photos of me as a baby.

The rock of doom had left me. Instead I felt empty.

Four single-serving boxes of Mega Flakes weren't enough to fill the howling emptiness of not being a true member of the family.

I slapped the empty book shut. A scrap of paper flew out from between the pages and floated to the floor. An old newspaper clipping. Probably something about Jessie winning the Most Beautiful Baby competition or Granddad winning a ribbon for his prize pumpkin. I didn't know which page the scrap came from, so I shoved it in my pocket.

I grabbed the next album off the shelf and flipped it open.

- Jessie's first school photo.
- Jessie dressed as a pirate, missing a tooth.

I flipped the page.

At last, a picture of me. I was standing by the kitchen table with my hands in the air. Mom had written *I can walk!* underneath it.

In the photo I wasn't a baby. I was already a toddler.

I kept turning the pages. There I was:

- Riding my kiddie car, knees up to my chin.
- In a child seat on the back of Dad's bike, my feet dragging on the ground.
- At the beach, using my cone of soft-serve ice cream as sunscreen while the rest of the family ate theirs.

In every photo I was getting older and taller.

The other albums were the same, chock-full of photos of Jessie and me growing up. The albums for the last two years included pictures of Timmy.

In one photo of the three of us, Jessie and Timmy looked like twins with an age gap — blond hair, blue eyes, smiling. I was standing apart from them, scowling.

My hair was different from theirs, and I never smiled for photos. I looked like a neighbor dragged along on a Kendal family outing.

There was absolutely no photographic record of Baby

Daniel—me. In a family where photos were taken all the time, that could mean only one thing.

I wasn't part of this family when I was a baby. I was born somewhere else.

I must have been adopted.

# 4

## The Truth About Me and My Life

I left the house to walk to school. But I couldn't walk, I trudged. The photographic truth weighed me down so I couldn't lift my feet off the sidewalk. I wasn't a true Kendal.

"Nice socks!" the mailman said.

I looked down at my ankles to see what he meant.

I like to get dressed in the dark. That way I don't have to look at myself. Who wants to be reminded first thing in the morning that they're too tall to be normal? Unfortunately, I had put on the socks Jessie gave me as a sick Christmas joke. Black with big pink hearts. The worst socks ever.

A construction worker whistled from the top of some high scaffolding.

"Nice socks!" he shouted.

I was going to be massacred when I got to school.

Weird socks are *not* cool. I ducked behind a trash container and raided my backpack for a black felt-tip. Then I colored in the hearts so it looked like I was wearing black socks below my too-short jeans. Unfortunately, the black pen rubbed off onto my skin, so it looked like I hadn't washed for a week. The black felt pen didn't smell, though, and I hoped no one would notice.

If Mom bought me jeans that fit, the whole "nice socks" thing would go away. But obviously I wasn't as important to her as her other kids, the ones she gave birth to.

I managed to get into my classroom without any more socks comments. Eddie was already there.

"I have a good one for you today, Dan my man," Eddie said. "Ready for the Toxic Samurai? Stand back—I could accidentally kill you."

Eddie is always trying to impress me with his extreme personal habits.

He tensed his body and raised his hands in a defensive kung fu position, his potato-chip bag clenched between his teeth. He scowled and went cross-eyed.

"Get on with it, buddy," I said. "Mr. Pitdown's going to walk in any minute." Mr. Pitdown is our teacher. He's not impressed by Eddie's performances.

Eddie hopped up and down on one foot and lashed out with the other leg, spinning his whole body around. As he whizzed past, he let out an enormous fart. Then his foot caught under a chair, throwing it into the air. It sailed over his head and toward a huddle of girls whispering and giggling.

"Watch out!" Rooners, the superjock, shouted as he

launched himself at the girls, shoving them out of the way.

The flying chair rebounded off the wall and flew toward the front of the room. The legs got tangled in a piece of string suspending a globe of the world from the ceiling. The world and the chair came crashing down onto Mr. Pitdown's desk.

"How's that?" he panted.

"Toxic," I said. I gave him a thumbs-up.

"*Fan*-tastic!" Eddie said as he crumpled the bag of his early-morning potato-chips and threw it in the trash. "Class photo today! I forgot my comb. Do you think anyone will notice?" He slid his salty, greasy fingers through his hair.

"Nah," I said. "Looks normal."

Eddie never worried about stuff like washing his hair. I could see a few potato-chip crumbs up there. I didn't say anything, because if he tried to get rid of them, the teachers would think he was picking out lice. I didn't want Eddie to be sent home from school with a lice letter today. I had important adoption stuff to discuss with him.

"Great T-shirt, by the way," he said, and slapped me on the shoulder.

T-shirt? I'd been so hung up on the sock problem, I hadn't checked what T-shirt I'd chosen in the darkness. I looked down at my chest. The T-shirt I was wearing had WORLD'S NUMBER ONE DAD printed across it. One of Dad's shirts, not mine.

"I'm not ready to be a father yet," I said.

"Try this one for size." Eddie pulled a brand-new T-shirt out of his school bag. "Dad got a shipment." Eddie's dad runs a discount store, and Eddie has inherited his knack for always having exactly the right thing at the right time. And lucky for me, Eddie likes to share.

"Thanks." I took the wrapped-up T-shirt.

Rooners bellowed that Mr. Pitdown wanted us to go to the gym for the photo.

"Come on. The evil photographer awaits." My number-one best friend disappeared into the hallway.

I dashed into the boys' bathroom to change. I didn't need any of the jocks making a joke about my body. Gordon, a.k.a. Gordon the Geek, my second-best friend, stood in front of the mirror adjusting his necktie. I didn't want to look at my scrawny self. I turned my back on the mirror and on my friend to change.

Gordon the Geek is the only kid in class who wears

a necktie. He wears it with a real shirt that has a collar, every single day. But Eddie and I let him hang out with us because he has lots of cool gadgets and lets us fool with them if we wash our hands first.

Eddie thought Gordon might be a very short adult spy disguised as a kid. I didn't agree. Gordon was just a geek with terrible taste in clothes.

Also, Gordon had a nasty habit of speaking the truth, the whole truth, and nothing but the truth. So I didn't think he could be a spy. Spies have to be very good at keeping secrets.

"Good morning," Gordon said.

"Nightmare," I said, and dumped Dad's shirt in the trash.

As I pulled on the new T-shirt, the door to the hallway flew open and our teacher came in.

"Gordon. Daniel. Gym, now!" Mr. Pitdown shouted.

Gordon took one more look in the mirror and flicked an invisible speck off his blazer.

"Very sharp," Mr. Pitdown purred as Gordon left the room.

Then he looked me up and down and muttered something under his breath. It sounded like "Where did that come from?" Of course he was talking about me like I wasn't a person.

Even though I wasn't the World's Number-One Dad anymore, Mr. Pitdown, the weirdest teacher at school, could see I didn't fit in.

# 5

# Photographs — Who Needs Them?

The other kids in my class were already in the gym, sitting in chairs on risers. For some reason, they all started laughing when I walked in.

I took the closest empty seat. Front row, far left. Eddie was somewhere in the middle, a million miles away from me. Gordon was sitting at the other end of my row.

"Hey, you! The abnormally tall one with the T-shirt!" the photographer shouted. "Back row, please."

I slouched down in my seat, trying to be less abnormal. I didn't know why he was picking on me. I wasn't the only kid wearing a T-shirt.

"Back row! You're ruining the shot." The photographer waved a laser pointer at me. I stood up and shuffled around to the back of the scaffolding.

"I'm not sure I can . . ." I looked up at the empty seat in the back row. "That's high."

"Daniel, back row. Now!" Mr. Pitdown shouted.

I started to climb. The whole class groaned as I scrambled over them to join the boys way up in the back row. I swear those risers were made of jelly or something. The higher I climbed, the more unstable they became.

By the time I was at the top, the room was one great shimmering hologram. Nothing solid. Nothing real. I grabbed hold of something to steady myself. The something screamed, and when I looked down, I realized I had my hands full of a girl's hair.

"Daniel, leave Susan alone!" Mr. Pitdown shouted.

The class burst out laughing.

"It's no good. Your head sticks way up." The photographer waved his red dot all over my face as if he was trying to erase me. "Come and lie down at the front." He drew a red laser line across the feet of the front row.

The minute my feet touched the floor, the wobbly feeling in my guts was replaced with a heavy feeling of doom. Lying at the feet of my classmates was a bad idea. Someone in the front row only had to twitch and they'd kick me.

I hoped Eddie would do something to rescue me. But the best-friend telepathy wasn't working. Eddie just grinned, stroked his top lip (which is our code for "Mr. Pitdown is a jerk"), and gave me a thumbs-up.

I raised an eyebrow at Gordon, at the end of the front row, hoping for a show of solidarity, but he ignored me. His eyes were focused on the camera, and he was ready to have his photo taken. Gordon always does exactly as he's told.

I lay down, with a class full of sixth-grade feet two inches away. I put my head in front of Gordon's feet. He was the only person I could trust not to kick me. Gordon doesn't do touching.

"What is that on your legs?" Mr. Pitdown said.

My jeans had ridden up, so everyone could see the dirty felt-tip marks on my calves.

"Mr. Pitdown, I can't sit here," the girl sitting by my ankles said. "I've got my best shoes on and my mom will kill me if I get them ruined." She pulled her feet up and hid them under her skirt.

"Daniel Kendal!" Mr. Pitdown shouted. "Out in the hall, now! And take your trash with you." He pointed at the scrap of newspaper that had fallen out of my pocket.

I stood out in the hallway while the sadist photographer made everyone say "cheese" ten thousand times.

That's when I looked down and saw what was on the T-shirt Eddie had given me. It said I ♥ above a picture of a giant mustache exactly like Mr. Pitdown's. *Thanks, pal!* I snarled telepathically. I was about to crumple the newspaper clipping and slam-dunk it in the trash can when I noticed the date printed at the top corner.

April 25. My birthday. The day I was born.

I smoothed out the paper to see what had been so important that Mom had kept the clipping in with the family photos.

# METEOR CRASHES TO EARTH IN PARK

Police have been inundated with reports of a possible meteor crashing to Earth in local Park Hill Fields. Investigators are mystified by a large crater that has appeared in the middle of the football field, but no evidence of the meteor itself has been found. They speculate that fragments of something from outer space may have been removed by meteor hunters. A Defense Department spokesperson says that it is highly unlikely to have been an alien spaceship crash-landing on Earth.

It happened on my birthday. Mom kept the newspaper clipping because it was about me.

My head buzzed with a billion thoughts. I tried to line them up so they made sense.

Jessie said I was an alien.

Alien spaceship landed.

Baby alien inside.

Mom and Dad pulled alien baby from crashed ship.

Dad put remains of spaceship in a Dumpster.

Mom took alien baby (me!) home.

They decided to keep me.

Baby alien became Daniel Kendal.

Mom kept newspaper clipping to remind her of how I came to be in this world.

Jessie was right.

I wasn't just adopted.

I was an alien.

No wonder I didn't fit in. No wonder they didn't want me in the class photo. I'd tried being human my whole life but I'd been wasting my time. A shiver went up and down my extra-long body as my brain took in the truth. I was a different species. One that didn't belong on Earth.

I was the ultimate misfit.

I was an alien.

*＊＊＊*

Mr. Pitdown called me back into the gym. "Individual portraits now, Daniel. I hope you are going to behave."

I nodded. My inner alien wanted to tell him I hadn't done anything wrong. But years of human experience told me not to bother arguing.

I got on the end of the line.

"These portraits are going to be very important." Mr. Pitdown was addressing the whole class. "We are going to create a Wall of Wonders in the classroom."

"What's that?" Susan asked.

"I'm going to put up all your portraits on the classroom wall. Whenever you do a particularly good piece of work or are picked for a sports team, I will post a commendation under your picture." Mr. Pitdown rolled the tip of his mustache between his finger and thumb. "In addition, you can add personal messages to your friends' pictures. At the end of the year, all of you will have a memento of your last year at this school."

"Cool!" The Jock Squad bumped each other's fists and whooped.

The girls huddled in groups and whispered.

I didn't want to have my photo taken with these

humans. I had nothing in common with them. I didn't need anything to remind me of my last year at this human school.

As I edged closer to the photographer, an epic idea started forming in my head. The emptiness in my stomach changed into a warm fuzziness. A feeling of certainty. A feeling of strength. At last I knew who I was.

I planted myself on the chair in front of the camera.

"Too tall!" the photographer said.

"You could adjust your tripod," I said.

"I really need individual pictures of the whole class," Mr. Pitdown said. "Daniel, kneel down." He pointed to a spot on the floor.

The kids snickered. Eddie shoved his hand up his sweater and armpit-farted the theme from *Mission: Impossible*.

Humans enjoy humiliating species from other planets. Even human best friends.

I sank to my knees.

"Smile!" the photographer said.

I put on my most demented alien face and made a decision.

*Click!* The photographer took the shot.

Mom could stick the photo in her album if she wanted to. It was going to be the last picture ever taken of me on Earth.

I didn't belong here. I needed to return to wherever I came from.

The alien known as Daniel Kendal was going home.

# 6

## Assembling the Mission Team

"Are you crazy?" Eddie said at recess.

He was supposed to be my best friend, but when I told him my earthshattering news, he didn't believe me.

"I'm an alien," I said. "It explains everything."

"Like what?"

I listed everything I could think of. The stuff I already mentioned, plus some new evidence.

| MY FAMILY'S FAVORITE THINGS | MY FAVORITE THINGS |
|---|---|
| Coffee | Chocolate milkshake with bacon bits |
| Toast | Baked beans |
| Lying in the sun (sometimes naked) | Hiding in the dark (always fully dressed) |

Eddie looked at me as if I was the biggest dork on the planet.

"Maybe your family doesn't like your chocolate-shake combo because it's disgusting. I wouldn't eat it," he said, stuffing potato chips in his mouth.

"That's because you're human and I'm not," I said. "I'm telling you, I don't fit into my family, and I certainly don't fit in around here. I'm not even in the class photo. I must be from somewhere else. Besides, my favorite candy is flying saucers." That was a lie. Flying saucers are UFO-shaped candies made of rice paper and filled with fizzy powder. I'd never eaten one, but Eddie didn't need to know that.

"I've never seen you eat flying saucers," Eddie said.

"I don't eat them because I want to fly in them," I said. I turned to my second-best friend. "You believe in aliens, don't you?"

Gordon the Geek was glued to his laptop as usual. He'd fastened a strap on it and hung it around his neck. It made him look like he was selling something from a tray.

"I'm an alien. Do you believe me?" I waved my hand in front of Gordon's face, being careful not to touch him.

"Cosmic," he replied, but he wasn't listening. He didn't look up, and his fingers kept moving over the keys as we walked across the playground.

Eddie and I had to guide him everywhere. We could

have led him straight into an open manhole or the cracks of doom and he'd never have known. But at least he'd die happy.

"If you are an alien, which planet are you from?" Eddie asked.

I didn't know the answer.

Eddie ripped open his potato-chip bag and licked the inside. He folded the wet bag into a paper airplane, but before he could fly it, the plastic had flopped open into a ripped potato-chip bag again.

He'd tried to make an airplane out of a potato-chip bag every day since school began. It never worked.

Gordon looked up. His eyes blinked furiously as he adjusted to the big wide world rather than the eleven-inch virtual world he'd been glued to. "Kepler 22b," he said.

"Are you sure?" I said.

"Kepler 22b. Two point four times the size of Earth. Probable surface temperature seventy-two degrees Fahrenheit. Six hundred light years away."

"What's that in English?" Eddie gets fed up with Gordon sometimes. Luckily, Gordon doesn't seem to mind. Otherwise I'd only have one friend on this planet.

"Approximately thirty-six hundred trillion miles from Earth. It's the answer to global warming. When this planet explodes, that's where we're heading." Gordon turned his laptop around and showed me a screen. It was a page from some scientific news service. It had a video showing what the scientist thought Kepler 22b looked like.

It was amazing. I'd never heard of Kepler 22b before, but now that planet was calling to me.

"So you mean there is a planet out there with aliens on it?" Eddie squinted at the screen.

"I don't suppose they consider themselves aliens when they're there." Gordon opened an online dictionary.

"Alien—a nonnaturalized foreigner, a being from another world.' Kepler 22b is home to them. They're not aliens there. Humans would be alien to the inhabitants of that planet."

The way they are to me.

# 7

# When Is an Alien Not an Alien?

I thought I'd be happy if I could get back to Kepler 22b.
I did have a few burning questions that needed answers:

- Did chocolate exist on Kepler 22b?
- What did an alien bike look like?
- Was a high-five a suitable alien greeting?

It was really important that I fit in the minute I got
there. I wouldn't be an alien or a misfit or a beanpole. For
once I'd be normal. I'd be a . . .

"What do you think the inhabitants of Kepler 22b call
themselves?" I asked the mission crew while we lined up
for lunch.

"Fries, please," Eddie said to the lunch lady.

"Keplerites?" I said. "What do you think, Gordon?"

Gordon the Geek lined up for lunch with Eddie and me every day. He rested his laptop and his briefcase on a tray and shoved the tray along the cafeteria rail while we talked, but he never ate anything. He thought school food was contaminated.

"Kepler is the name of the telescope that spotted the planet," Gordon said.

"So Kepler is a human word?"

Gordon looked at me over the top of his glasses like a fed-up professor. "Yes. Kepler is a human word. There are only human words, because we don't know any aliens or how they speak."

"You know me," I said.

"But you weren't an alien until yesterday," Eddie said. He rolled his eyeballs so far back into his head, he must have been looking at his brain. If he had one.

"Yes, I know you," Gordon said. "But you were brought up by humans and speak human. English, actually. I guess you could call it a dialect of human speech."

"Do you think the inhabitants of Kepler 22b have different languages?" A meteor of panic hit me hard in the stomach. "What if I finally get to meet some of them and they come from North Kepler 22b and I came from South Kepler 22b and I can't understand a word they're saying?"

"Mr. Kendal, do you speak any language other than English?" Gordon only calls me Mr. Kendal when he's bored.

"No."

"So if some Spanish girl walked in now and spoke to you, you wouldn't understand her. Right?" Gordon said.

Eddie smirked. "I'd understand every word."

I turned my back on Eddie and slammed my tray onto the table. I felt like slamming it on my best friend's head.

"I'd understand any kid if they pointed to the food and used sign language," I said to Gordon.

"There you go," said Gordon. "You're going to have to make do with sign language if you ever meet anyone from Kepler 22b. Because you won't be able to understand them unless they speak English."

Gordon was right. I was an idiot. I knew only one language.

I should have elected to study a foreign language. Our school offered German, French, and Spanish, not Alien, but the more languages you know, the easier it is to understand a non-English speaker.

I could still sign up for Italian club. But it was a bit late. I needed to get to Kepler 22b right now.

During lunch period, Mr. Pitdown printed out the portraits and created the Wall of Wonders. By the end of the day, most of the portraits had personal messages added to them. Things like *BFF* and sparkly stickers on the girls' photos, *Greatest pitcher* and *Cool shirt* on the boys'.

Someone wrote *Most kissable mouth* under Eddie's photo. Eddie ate too many potato chips, and he had some disgusting personal habits, but he has amazing teeth. They are perfectly straight. Other comments under Eddie's photo:

- *Nice mouth. Shame about the face.*
- *And the smell.*
- *Ditto.*
- *Fart Master* (this was added in Eddie's handwriting).

My photo was completely blacked out with a felt-tip marker. No one had written anything on it. I tried to clean the marker off, but Mr. Pitdown said not to bother.

I suggested I take the picture home to see if Dad could clean it up. But Mr. Pitdown muttered that he hadn't intended to open a new path to bullying. He needn't have worried—aliens like me are used to that sort of thing —but he took the whole Wall of Wonders down and returned the pictures and comments to each person in the class. He forgot to print a fresh photo for me to take home. Either that or he decided I didn't deserve one, as I was only an alien.

# 8

## I Am a Long Way from Home

The persecution on Earth was getting me down. I needed to get back to Kepler 22b ASAP. But I couldn't do it on my own.

I invited my only friends over for a secret meeting.

Eddie, Gordon, and I always hung out at my house. Gordon wouldn't let us into his home, because he didn't like to have his personal space invaded. Eddie's house was so full of brothers, cousins, uncles with girlfriends, babies, and grandparents, we'd never get a minute to ourselves.

- Place: Timmy's playhouse
- Address: Middle of Kendal family backyard
- Advantage: No one can overhear us outdoors. My bedroom has very thin walls.
- Disadvantage: Place is on the small side.

Timmy's playhouse was supposed to be a den for a single two-year-old, not three sixth-grade boys—one with abnormally long alien legs, another with disgusting personal habits, and another with a touching phobia and a laptop.

"Is it clean?" Gordon asked, leaning down to peer through the tiny door.

The playhouse was empty except for Timmy's red chair. I'd scrubbed off a smear of strawberry jam and a squashed graham cracker before they arrived.

"One hundred percent sterile," I said.

Gordon zapped the playhouse inside and out with disinfectant spray and wiped down Timmy's chair a hundred times before he sat on it. His knees came up nearly to his chin, but there was just room for his laptop as long as he undid the strap. There was no room to revive him if the strap got pulled tight and strangled him. And anyway, mouth-to-mouth resuscitation would kill Gordon for sure.

Eddie bounded across the lawn hugging a huge plastic bag.

"Got something for you." He thrust the bag into my arms.

It was a sack of flying saucers.

"Thanks," I said.

"Open it," Eddie said. "Maybe if you eat enough, the fizzy stuff will produce enough gas to lift you off this planet."

I didn't want to admit to Eddie that I'd lied about flying saucers being my favorite candy, so I put one in my mouth. It tasted of paper. I bit down, and a saccharine fizz spread up my nose and made my eyes water.

"Epic!" I announced, hoping I sounded convincing. Eddie was only trying to help.

Eddie shoved his hand into the bag and pulled out a handful of candies. He shoved them into his mouth, chewed for a few seconds, and then coughed them onto Dad's lawn.

"Gross!" he said. "You must be from another planet if you like them." Eddie stuck his finger in his mouth and pried out a glob of stuck-together rice paper. He flicked it into the hedge.

A geeky voice came from the playhouse. "Hello? This meeting is officially ten minutes late."

"Stand back, I'm coming in." Eddie shoved his right foot through the playhouse door.

"Before you do that," I said, "you have to swear."

"No problem," Eddie said. He spouted an impressive

string of bad words, ending with one that sounded sort of like "Zakryxkekny!"

"Where did you get that one from?"

"Made it up," Eddie said. "Sounds good, doesn't it?"

"Yeah, but I didn't mean that kind of swearing." I held up a dictionary. It was the most official-looking book I could find. "Stick your hand on that and read this." I'd written a solemn oath on a card for him.

Eddie laughed. "Are you serious?"

"You have to swear, or you're off the mission team."

Eddie snorted, but he put his hand on the dictionary and chanted, "I, Eddie, do solemnly promise that I will not fart"—he started to crack up—"in the meeting."

"Thanks," I said, and put the card away. I decided to keep the dictionary with me in case Gordon used long words during the meeting.

Eddie has eaten so many potato chips over the years that he's rather large, and I'm taller than the human inhabitants of this planet, so it took us ten minutes to squeeze ourselves into the playhouse.

I stuck my legs out the window so they didn't touch Gordon accidentally.

Eddie sat in the doorway, his butt sticking out. Just

in case. "Consider me an early-warning system," he said. "I'll let one off if anyone approaches."

"No!" Gordon tried to get up, but he couldn't move without touching us.

I tried to hit Eddie over the head with the dictionary, but it was wedged between my elbow and my right ear.

"Only joking," Eddie said. "But get started—I can't hold it in forever. I had beans last night."

I would never hold another mission meeting in Timmy's playhouse. And I'd find out what Eddie had for dinner before I invited him over.

"All good missions need a mission statement," I said. "How about 'I need to return to Kepler 22b'?"

"That's not a mission statement. That's your crazy dream," Eddie said.

"'To return the alien known as Daniel Kendal to Kepler 22b,'" Gordon said.

"Good one," I said.

"Are you sure you're an alien?" Eddie asked. "Maybe you're adopted."

"Of course I'm adopted. I'm an alien, aren't I? My parents aren't my parents. They're human."

"Maybe you're an adopted human from another human family."

Eddie was really beginning to bug me. Why couldn't he accept me for what I was?

"I am not human. I am an alien. Jessie told me, and my parents have been trying to keep the secret from me forever. *That's* why I don't fit in here. And that's why I *need* to get back to my home planet." The smell of Eddie's cheese-and-onion breath and his bad attitude were getting on my nerves. "How am I going to get back to Kepler 22b?"

Eddie stuck his finger in his mouth and came out with another wad of soggy flying saucer. He rolled it between his finger and thumb.

"Don't—" Before I could finish the sentence, he'd flicked the flying saucer/spit wad at the ceiling.

He winked.

I would have poked his stupid winking eye out if I could have reached it without touching Gordon.

"You're going to have to go into hibernation if you want to arrive on Kepler 22b alive." Gordon looked up from his laptop, unaware that a flying saucer time bomb infected with Eddie's germs hung two inches above his head. His eyes wandered around in their sockets before fixing their gaze on me. "It's so far away."

I dragged my eyes away from the time bomb and tried to concentrate on what Gordon was saying.

"Hibernation? How do I do that?"

"Cryogenics. You'll need to be frozen alive."

I didn't like the sound of that, but I knew Gordon was

right. The journey to Kepler 22b was a long one, and I didn't want to be an old man when I got there. I wanted to be a normal Keplerite kid. To go to a school where I fit in. I wanted to buy a Keplerite smartphone, and maybe even start dating a Keplerite girl after a few years.

"So how does this cryogenics thing work?" I said.

"We're going to need a lot of ice."

# 9

# The Most Awesome Plan Ever

By the end of the meeting, I knew exactly what I needed to do to get to Kepler 22b.

### MISSION STATEMENT

To return the alien known as Daniel Kendal to Kepler 22b.

### PREPARATION AND TRAINING

1. Test cryogenic survival, a.k.a. being frozen alive.

2. Find country with plans to relocate to Kepler 22b.

3. Raise cash for airfare to foreign country.

4. Get fit. Astronauts have to be in peak physical condition.

5. Pack stuff to take to new planet:

   • Handheld games console and charger

- Backup handheld games console and charger

- All games for games console and backup games console

- Three latest *Simpsons Comics* to read while waiting for takeoff

6. Things to trade with Kepler kids to make friends:

- Deadly Venomous Snakes cards

- Dinosaur stickers

- Plastic yo-yos and harmonicas

"With stuff like that, I'm going to be really popular on Kepler 22b," I said as I ended the meeting.

"What makes you think any kid wants a cheap yo-yo that doesn't work? You'd be better off taking a MegaYo or a YoYammer," Eddie said. "Anyway, what happens to a yo-yo in zero gravity?"

"It floats around like a helium balloon," Gordon said.

"They have gravity on Kepler 22b." I was getting fed up with Eddie spoiling my plans. "It's a planet, isn't it?"

"I'm out of here," Eddie said. He wrapped his arm around his head and twisted his body in an attempt to leave the tiny playhouse headfirst.

I didn't know if it was Eddie's escape attempt or my shouting, but the rice-paper time bomb was on the move. A ball bearing of mush was now dangling from the ceiling on a fine wet thread, and the gap between it and the Geek's head was closing.

I needed Gordon. If he got contaminated, he'd leave the mission. Without Gordon I'd be stuck on Earth forever. Eddie was ruining everything.

"They probably don't have yo-yos on Kepler 22b," I shouted at Eddie as he tried to wiggle free. "The alien kids will have their own things to trade, and my Earth collectibles will be so rare that they'll give me loads of Keplerite stuff in exchange. My black mamba card is particularly awesome. It's worth a Keplerite smartphone all by itself."

Eddie grunted as he flung his body toward the grass outside. His legs flew up, his heel caught the roof of the playhouse, and with a screech of plastic the roof flew into the air, taking the wad of rice paper with it. Without the roof, the playhouse started to collapse.

Gordon screamed and hid his head in his laptop.

The walls of the playhouse skewed out of position, and for a moment Gordon and I were sitting in a diamond-shaped playhouse with no roof. The sky looked very big and blue.

The plastic lugs holding the walls together wrenched from their sockets, and the house caved in on us.

"Arghhh!" Gordon scrabbled to get a can out of his briefcase. He sprayed himself from head to toe with disinfectant. "Don't ask me to get into an enclosed space with Eddie ever again," he said.

"No problem. The plan is set." I waved my notebook in the air. "Kepler 22b, here I come!"

# 10

## The Truth About Cryogenics

Gordon said I had to be naked to be frozen alive.

I disagreed. I did not have the Kendal nudist DNA in my blood.

The mission team was crammed into the Kendal family bathroom while the rest of the Kendal family was at a barbecue next door. We had two hours to achieve absolute zero.

"Clothing will act as an insulator," Gordon said. "Basic science."

"Clothing is important to Keplerites like me," I said.

"What's the problem?" Eddie said. "Get naked!"

"No way!" I pulled up my hoodie and drew my fists into my sleeves.

"Are you serious about wanting to get back to Kepler 22b?" Eddie asked. "Because I'm a bit concerned that you're not really taking this seriously."

That's the kind of friend Eddie is. Totally sarcastic.

I went back to my room and came out wearing my bathing suit.

"I don't think I need cryogenics," I said. Rubbing my hands over my arms didn't make the mega goose bumps go away. I hate being cold, but Dad won't let us put the heat on during the day. That was another reason why I knew I was an alien. The surface temperature of Kepler 22b was 72°F, much warmer than my human home on Earth. I didn't belong here.

"How much ice do we have?" Gordon asked.

- My contribution: three ice cube trays with eighteen cubes in each, for a total of fifty-four cubes.
- Eddie's contribution: eight supersize bags of ice packed in his gran's shopping cart.
- Gordon's contribution: a thermos.

"The Cryogenics Practitioner's Secret Ingredient," he said, holding the thermos up. "Now is the time to tell us if you've changed your mind." An evil-scientist's grin spread across his face as he pulled on a pair of surgical gloves. He was loving this—experimenting on a real live alien. Some kids like setting fire to things, others like blowing stuff up. For Gordon, freezing me solid was the big thrill.

For me, freezing me solid was just one challenging step on the road to Kepler 22b.

"I haven't changed my mind," I said. "Get on with it." My human family was next door at Jessie's friends' barbecue. We now had less than two hours before they came home and someone started hammering on the bathroom door.

"Then I shall proceed." Gordon straightened his glasses and rolled up his sleeves. He shoved a thermometer under my tongue. It was lucky I didn't bite it—my chattering teeth were totally out of control. "Ninety-eight point six degrees Fahrenheit. Still normal."

*For a human,* I thought.

"Shall I put in the ice now?" Eddie said.

"Not yet," Gordon said. "We have to get his body temperature down in stages. Otherwise the shock could kill him."

Gordon was talking to Eddie, not me, which was very rude, but I couldn't say anything, as I had a glass tube stuck under my tongue. If I opened my jaws, my teeth would snap on the glass and break the thermometer in

two. If I swallowed glass fragments, I wouldn't need to go into cryostasis. I'd die of internal bleeding here on Earth.

Mission failed.

Maybe it was a good thing the best-friend telepathy wasn't working, because my brain was screaming at me not to do it.

Eddie and Gordon looked at me expectantly.

If I backed out now, the mission would be over, and I would be stuck in my unhappy life on Earth forever. I looked at the chilly bath water. Which was worse?

The moment had come.

I stepped into the bathtub.

Ice or no ice, it was freakin' freezing. My feet instantly turned ice blue, and a rash of goose bumps charged up my body, making my few body hairs stand on end. It was probably my body's instinctive attempt to keep me warm, but it was failing. I was sure my temperature had dropped twenty degrees instantly.

"No change yet," Gordon said. "Time to submerge. We have to get that temperature down. Otherwise your body will melt the ice rather than ice freezing your internal organs solid."

I'd never taken a bath in cold water before. I wrapped my tongue around the thermometer, clenched my lips together, and sank my shivering body into the water.

I didn't know cold water could hurt. From the waist down, my poor Keplerite body was gripped in a chilly vise.

"Lie down! Lie down!" Gordon the Geek, my second-best friend, put his hands on my shoulders and pushed me backward. The icy water lapped over my chest, ending in a stranglehold around my neck. Only my head and bent knees were out of the water. My head because I was supposed to be freezing, not drowning, and my knees because I'm too tall to lie flat in the tub.

"Freakin' freezing," I said. What with the thermometer and my chattering teeth, it sounded like "frnknnnrng freeezzzrng."

"You've got a long way to go yet." Gordon checked the thermometer. "Still ninety-eight point six degrees."

"No!" I shook my head vigorously, willing the line to slip farther down the tube. Surely my body temperature had dropped enough by now.

"How long does he have to stay in there?" Eddie asked. He was playing with a piece of dental floss. He'd wrapped it around each of his teeth in turn so it looked like white string braces. Not that he needed braces, with his great teeth and "most kissable mouth."

"Ages," Gordon said. "There is no change in temperature yet."

He had to be wrong. I had absolutely no feeling in my body. I was already well on the way to cryostasis.

"Maybe we should let this water out and fill up with colder water from the tap?" Eddie said.

Gordon put his hand in the bath water and yanked it out superquick.

"No need. It's still cold." He peered at the thermometer again. "Aha! It's down to ninety-seven degrees at last. Eddie — the ice!" he said triumphantly.

He didn't ask me if I still wanted to be frozen alive. I didn't know the answer anyway. I didn't know much about anything anymore. Even though my head wasn't under the water, my brain had already turned into a zombie's ice pop.

My two best friends stood over me and dumped ice into the tub.

I had ice between my toes. Ice crammed under my armpits. Ice piled up on my chest.

My knees stuck up above the sea of mini icebergs. Eddie draped bags stuffed with slushy ice over those last bits of visible skin and another bag over my head.

They didn't pile ice on top of my swimming trunks. I guess they realized the contents had already gone into hibernation.

Gordon held his thermos in front of my face. I nodded. He took off the lid. Smoke curled up from the opening. Whatever the Cryogenics Practitioner's Secret Ingredient was, I was ready for it.

Gordon poured something in the gap between my frozen feet at the bottom of the bathtub.

A cloud of billowing smoke erupted over the surface of the water. It spread out over my chest and head, engulfing me completely. The temperature of the freezing bath water dropped another zillion degrees, squeezing the last warm breath out of my body.

My jaw dropped open. The thermometer dangled from my iceberg lip. I breathed in the weird dry smoke that didn't smell of anything. The chill entered my lungs and spread through my body from the inside out.

Then a really weird thing happened. Instead of feeling cold, I started feeling warm. My teeth stopped chattering, and the surface of my body glowed hot as if I was wearing some sort of fiery onesie. Maybe being cryogenically frozen wasn't so bad after all.

My brain and my body weren't on the same planet anymore. My brain was on Kepler 22b, my body somewhere else a million miles away. In the space in between, a geeky kid peered into my face. I knew him from somewhere. His glasses were familiar. A knobby hand reached out and turned the weird tube sticking out of my mouth.

"Ninety-five degrees. It's working." His mouth cracked open, and I could see a row of teeth and a pink tongue.

"Show me," another familiar voice said.

I was aware of someone with a mouth full of string.

64

I might have known him once.

A voice cackled. Another howled. Only there weren't two of them now. There were two, four, eight, sixty-four. The faces multiplied rapidly, until all I could see was a million cackling idiots.

Then, just like his portrait on the Wall of Wonders, the alien known as Daniel Kendal blacked out.

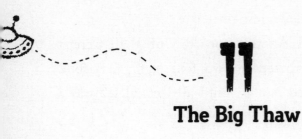

# The Big Thaw

"Wake up! Wake up!" Something solid hit my face, and my cheeks exploded with ten thousand volts of pain.

Something rough rubbed over my arms and legs, turning them into zinging electrified eels.

"Hand me those hot-water bottles." A fluffy warmth was pressed under my armpits.

"Wake up! Do you think we should call an ambulance?"

These were the words I heard, but I can't remember what order they came in. Blurry faces, lots of shouting, and the excruciating pain of heat applied to my cryogenically frozen body.

These Keplerites were expert at defrosting their species, *and* they spoke English. Somewhere in among the ice crystals, I remembered thinking, *I've arrived.*

"Thank you," I said, even though I was in total agony.

"He's alive!" a voice shrieked. It sounded just like Mom. My human mom who had brought me up on Earth.

What was Mom doing on Kepler 22b? I thought I'd be the only alien around here.

I flickered my eyelids and checked out my home planet.

- *Doctor Who* posters on the wall.
- Battered Buzz Lightyear hanging from the ceiling.
- Stick collection on the windowsill.

That's when I realized I wasn't on Kepler 22b. I was in my bedroom. The one at 26 Beechwood Road on Earth.

I opened my eyes properly so I could be one hundred percent certain about that.

My human mom and dad stood by my bed. Mom with staring eyes. Dad's forehead lined with worry.

Hot blood thumped through my veins, defrosting my confusion.

I wasn't on Kepler 22b. Eddie, Gordon, and I were only trying out the freezing process. I hadn't made the journey yet. I *was* still on Earth. I hadn't gone anywhere.

"Daniel, look at me," Mom said, and slapped my face again.

"That's child abuse," I said.

"Thank goodness. He's back from the dead." She threw herself on me, smothering me with her hair. I didn't have the strength to push her away. It was pretty tragic that I had survived the deep freeze only to be suffocated by my human mother.

"I'm calling the child-abuse hotline," I said, spitting out a mouthful of hair.

"Hotline? They can't help you. It's a psychiatrist you need," Mom said.

"Calm down, Liz. Calm down," Dad said. "It was just a prank. Gordon and Ed said they were doing an experiment for science club."

"They nearly killed him!"

"They were trying to find out how long a body can survive in freezing water."

"Did they force you?" Mom patted my burning cheek.

"No," I said.

"If you're being bullied at school, I need to know about it."

"It was an experiment that went wrong."

"Don't they experiment on rats anymore?" Mom said.

"The ASPCA wouldn't like it," I murmured.

"You made yourself a giant guinea pig instead?"

"I think I need a nap now," I said. Mom's shrieks were giving my frozen brain a headache.

"Yes, of course." Mom patted my hand and I let out a guinea pig squeak. "I'm going to look up *hypothermia* on the computer, in case you need to be in the hospital."

"Where are Gordon and Eddie?" I said.

"Gone home! They aren't allowed in this house ever again!" Mom stormed out, banging the open door against the wall.

Alone at last. The experiment had worked. I could survive being frozen and defrosted, but I didn't want to do it too often. Next time would be the real thing. The day I shipped out to Kepler 22b.

We needed to move on to step two. How was I going to get to Kepler 22b?

# 12

# The Boy Who Came from Earth

Because Mom thought I'd nearly died, she said I should stay out of school for a week. She arranged to work from home and left Timmy at daycare so she could look after me.

But when she said I could stay home for a week, she meant I had to stay in bed. Freakin' boring! She gave me the bell from Jessie's bicycle and told me to ring it if I needed anything.

An hour later she took the bell downstairs, muttering about slavery.

Five Alien Activities to Do When Imprisoned
in Human Bed

1. Reread *Simpsons Comics*.
2. Reorganize Deadly Venomous Snakes cards.

3. Count the cracks in the ceiling.

4. Take a nap.

5. I can't think of another one.

By midafternoon I was ready to get up and start researching which countries had the technology to get me to Kepler 22b.

"Can I come down and use the computer?" I asked Mom when she came up with a snack.

"No. I need to do some work."

"Can I watch TV?"

"No. I can't concentrate if the TV is on."

My human mom is very fond of the word *no*.

"Why do we have the computer in the same room as the TV?" I said.

"Not again!" Mom sighed. "The computer lives in the family room because I like to know what you're doing on the computer."

"Why?"

Mom left the room without answering.

Human parents don't understand the basic needs of alien kids like me.

I bet kids on Kepler 22b had their own computers or some other alien technology. And they were going to share it with me. The Boy Who Came from Earth. They'd probably think I was exotic. They might even think I was cool. I thought Kepler 22b would be the coolest planet in the universe, and I kept thinking about all the cool stuff I'd find there.

My Wish List for Kepler 22b

1. A laptop wired into my brain, so I'd know everything without having to ask anyone.

2. A teleporter, so I could go anywhere instantly without having to walk.

3. A full set of fifty Deadly Venomous Aliens cards so I'd know who I could be friends with.

4. A telepathic phone so all I'd have to do was think *Eddie* and I'd be able to talk to him without opening my mouth.

5. A loft bed. I'd always wanted one, but Mom kept saying no.

I had to switch off my alien fantasy pretty quick when Jessie came in and plonked herself on the end of my Earth bed.

"You still here, Beanpole?" she said.

"Yes, but I'm not a beanpole. I'm an alien, remember?"

She looked puzzled for a moment, but then her lip-glossed mouth cracked into a smile. "You really have to meet Serena Blake."

"Who is Serena Blake?"

"She's in my class. Dyed black hair cut short. She says she was snatched into a spaceship by one of you guys, then dumped back on Earth when they'd finished with her."

"She's human, though, isn't she?"

"Yeah, but she has a thing about little green men.

Martians. The man in the moon. Whatever. She yaks about them all the time. She wants to go back to alien land and live there. She's nuts." Jessie stood up. "Mom says she's finished using the computer. But you can't use it, because I am." She poked her human tongue out and left, slamming the door, of course.

Jessie was the worst kind of human sister. The sooner I left this planet, the better, and that wasn't going to happen if I was chained to the bed. I needed my team and the Geek's technology to get me out of here.

"You need to stay home all week," Mom said when I went downstairs.

"But I'm not sick."

She held me by both hands and looked into my eyes.

"You nearly died," she said.

"If I was so near death, how come you didn't take me to the hospital?"

"I decided it was best to care for you at home," Mom said.

"It had nothing to do with wanting to stay at the barbecue?"

Mom blushed.

Cryostasis messes with your brain, but once you've

thawed out, the brain works perfectly. Mom and Dad thought I was still in the fuzzy phase of hypothermia when they had a fight about whether I should go to the hospital.

But I'd heard every word. And understood all of them.

Dad said, "He's sleeping now. We shouldn't disturb him."

Mom said, "But I'm worried."

Dad said, "If his lips are still blue in a couple of hours, we'll take him."

"Good thing I thawed out without dying, isn't it?" I picked up Jessie's bicycle bell from the kitchen table and rang it endlessly.

"You can go back to school tomorrow." Mom snatched the bell out of my hand and threw it in the trash.

# 13

## Teacher Spit and Other Problems

The desks in my classroom were grouped in pairs and lined up in three columns. Five pairs in each column. I sat next to Eddie, of course. He was my best friend, and no one else wanted to sit next to a long-legged alien or a potato-chip-encrusted fart monster.

But things had changed while I'd been in the deep freeze. Gordon was sitting in my seat next to Eddie. Gordon's usual seat was empty.

"What's going on?" I said.

"Wasn't sure you'd want to be friends anymore, since I nearly killed you," Eddie said, keeping his eyes focused on the inside of his potato-chip bag.

"You didn't nearly kill me. It was voluntary cryostasis."

"That's not what your mom said. She went on and on about me bullying you into doing it. She told the school we're not allowed to sit next to each other because I might try to kill you again." He bent down to tie his shoelaces. He didn't seem to realize his sneakers had Velcro.

Thanks to Mom, I had to sit in the center aisle, front row, right next to a girl.

"Welcome back!" Mr. Pitdown shouted in a fake-cheery voice. I could tell by the evil glint in his eye that he wished I'd stayed at home.

At that moment I wished I was still at home too, instead of sitting at the desk closest to him and his spit spray.

I didn't know how Gordon had coped with sitting in the front row all year. No wonder he sprayed his whole desk with disinfectant at the start and end of every class.

"I'm pleased you've found your new seat, where I can keep an eye on you, make sure you're okay." Mr. Pitdown was talking loud enough for everyone to hear.

A snicker rippled through the class.

Oh, great! I'd been promoted from class misfit to class wimp. I plopped down in my new seat and glared at Mr. Pitdown. I'd been out of school for one day and I'd already lost my best friend. Now I had to sit in the front like a real dork.

"Hi," the girl next to me said. She pulled one of her

pigtails around the edge of her jaw and popped the end into her mouth.

"Sorry you were sick," she said. "Are you better now?"

"Hmph!" I said. I didn't want to break my personal rule about not speaking to girls (except my sister, who doesn't count).

Sitting in the front row is a total nightmare if you want to make plans to escape from this solar system. Mr. Pitdown was a pacer, the kind of teacher who strides back and forth as he talks. He probably didn't have time to go to the gym because of all the papers he had to grade, so he needed the exercise.

I'd heard other teachers complaining about how much time they spent grading papers. Didn't they realize that if they gave us easier work, we wouldn't make so many mistakes, and the grading wouldn't take so long? Thirty check marks would take less time to write than correcting 30 x 19 spelling mistakes and 30 x 67 punctuation errors, and writing thirty comments about students not having written enough.

Teachers can be amazingly clueless sometimes.

Anyway, Mr. Pitdown did his workout right there in the classroom. Today he even worked up a sweat, because every time he crossed the room, he had to jump over my

legs. The sweat dripped down to join the spittle on the edge of his mustache.

I'd have to bring an umbrella to school.

He walked back and forth and jumped over my legs so

often, I couldn't concentrate on how I was going to get to Kepler 22b.

At the end of the class, Mr. Pitdown made me change seats with Gordon again. He must have decided that it wasn't such a great idea to have a long-legged alien in the front row.

Now I could return to making my plans for getting out of here. I figured that three brains would be better than one. I decided to call another mission meeting.

# 14

## До ыоу спеак Руссиан?

Eddie, Gordon, and I met in the dark corner under the fire escape to discuss what to do next.

"We've figured out the cryostasis, sort of, but how am I actually going to get my frozen body up there?" I waved my hand in the direction of outer space.

Eddie stuffed a fistful of potato chips in his mouth and started munching.

Gordon was wearing his laptop as usual. He was totally focused on the screen as his fingers danced across the keys.

Once again the best-friend telepathy must have been faulty. My first- and second-best friends were not picking up my thoughts even when I went to the trouble of speaking.

"Hello? Is anyone listening to me?"

"Sure we're listening, but you're not saying much,"

Eddie said. He ripped open the empty potato-chip bag and licked the salt and grease from the inside.

"I'm looking for suggestions," I said.

"Join NASA, I guess."

"No point," Gordon said. "The space-shuttle program is over, and NASA only has plans to go to the International Space Station. You'll have to go to Russia."

"Russia?"

"Only way to get to space is via Russia." Gordon pushed his glasses up the bridge of his nose. "Unless China has a space program they're not telling us about, and if it's that secret, they aren't going to let you join, are they?"

I could always borrow a Russian-language course CD from the library.

"How do I get to Russia?" I asked.

"The next flight to Moscow leaves at three thirty," Gordon read from his computer screen. "But that won't leave you enough time to get through security. It's one o'clock now."

"Do you think if I show up at the Russian space agency and offer to go to Kepler 22b under cryostasis, they'll let me?"

"No!" Eddie said. He flicked his crumpled potato-chip bag at me.

"Why not?" Gordon said. "They aren't allowed to use animals anymore."

"Okay. How much is the airfare?"

Gordon turned his computer around and showed me a spreadsheet. First class: $6,000. Business class: $3,000. Economy: $500.

I pulled fifty-two cents out of my pocket. "How much money do you have?"

Eddie had $2.60, but he needed $1.75 for potato chips on his way home, so he only gave me eighty-five cents.

"Gordon?"

Gordon didn't flinch. He kept on tapping.

Have I mentioned that Gordon was stingy? He was my friend and everything, but he never had any money. At least we never saw him spend any. He didn't eat lunch, he didn't eat potato chips, and I'd never seen him drink anything but water.

Eddie and I had this theory that Gordon was saving up for something. He presumably got an allowance, and he did PC support for older people who didn't know how to use their computers. So he probably had a lot of money put away.

"Gordon, can you loan me the money to fly to Russia?"

"No," he said.

"I'll pay you back."

"No."

I could tell he was only pretending to look at his laptop. He was ignoring me.

If Gordon was an alien, he would have been able to read my thoughts and would know how important it was for me to get to Kepler 22b. But Gordon wasn't an alien, he was human, and he wasn't going to loan me the money, because he's so stingy. Granddad would say that Gordon is "tight as a frog's backside, and that's watertight."

I didn't need to create a spreadsheet to tell me I didn't have enough money to get to Russia.

I couldn't borrow it anyway, because there was probably no way of sending money back from Kepler 22b. And who knew what currency the Keplerites used.

"So how am I going to get the money for the flight to Russia?" I said.

There was an ominous silence.

Have you noticed there are very limited opportunities for kids to make money? I could do chores at home, but Mom and Dad only paid fifty cents per chore. It would take me eons to earn enough to go to Russia, and by that time I'd be an adult and would have missed spending my teenage years on Kepler 22b.

"Halloween's next week," Eddie said. "We could go trick-or-treating."

"What use is a bag of gummy skulls and a Tootsie Roll?" I said.

"We could get some awesome costumes," Eddie said, ignoring me.

"Jessie has a witch costume you can borrow," I said.

"Candy store," Gordon said.

There was a weird silence as Eddie and I tried to figure out how to go trick-or-treating dressed as a candy store.

"If we get enough trick-or-treat swag, we could open a candy store at recess and sell the candy to the other kids," Gordon explained.

Have I ever referred to Gordon as the Geek? I meant to call him *Gordon the Genius*.

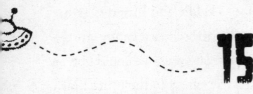

# 15

# The Great Halloween Transformation

First we had to get some awesome Halloween costumes. The better the costumes, the better the swag. No one was going to give us any candy if we were wearing lame sheets with holes for eyes.

I figured I could save money on a mask and go for face paint and a crazy hairstyle. The only good thing about having an older sister was that she had loads of makeup and hair gunk.

I couldn't make up my mind whether to dress up as a vampire or a werewolf.

| VAMPIRES | WEREWOLVES |
|---|---|
| Cool | Scary |
| Slicked-back hair (loads of gel required) | Scruffy fur (already have scruffy hair, so no gel required) |
| Only go out at night (okay, because trick-or-treating happens at night) | Can't go out at the full moon (need to check the moon on Halloween) |
| Might be mistaken for a dead person and buried alive | Might be mistaken for a rabid dog and shot by the police |

I had some plastic fangs that would work well for either a vampire or a werewolf, but I didn't know what to wear on the rest of me.

"What do werewolves wear?" I asked my family the morning of Halloween.

Mom and Dad both picked up their cups of coffee with their right hands and took a sip at exactly the same time. The way they are synchronized with each other freaks me out. They didn't answer.

"Werewolves don't exist," Jessie said.

"They do in movies."

"Movies aren't real," she said.

"Let me ask the question another way. If I dress up as a werewolf on Halloween, what should I wear?"

"Nothing. Werewolves lose their clothes when they transform, and they run around in their hairy naked bodies biting people." Jessie grinned. "Let me know when you're ready so I can take a photo and put it on Facebook. I've got 1,235 followers."

"You could get some furry mittens and stick a little fur at the opening of your shirt." Mom had joined the conversation. "Since you don't have any chest hair yet."

Why were my family obsessed with bodies—mine and theirs? They were totally unsympathetic to my

sensitive alien psyche. Aliens need to be dressed all the time.

I decided to go as Count Dracula. Count Dracula had really bad clothes sense, but he never went around naked.

After school I put on black jeans, Dad's old dinner jacket and dress shirt, and socks touched up with felt-tip marker so they looked black. I slicked back my hair with baby oil.

Then I sneaked into Jessie's room to rifle through her makeup. She didn't have white face paint. She had something called Instant Copper Bronze, but they must have put the wrong label on the tube, because when I squeezed some out onto my fingertips, it was white. I slapped it on really thickly. She had some red lipstick, and the way I put it on made it look like I'd just stuck my teeth into someone's jugular vein. I also managed to stab myself in the eye with an eyeliner pencil, and the bloodshot look added to the overall effect.

Count Dracula was ready.

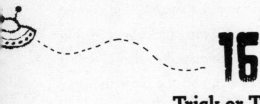

# 16

## Trick or Treat?

Eddie and Gordon still weren't allowed in my house, so they met me on the corner. I was totally unimpressed with their costumes.

"What's this?" I tugged at the sheet covering Gordon's head. He hadn't even bothered to cut eyeholes in it.

The sheet twitched as if the geek inside was shrugging. I could hear the tap of fingers on keys.

"Where's your costume?" I asked Eddie. He had on jeans and a hoodie as usual, but his face was in shadow. He turned suddenly, and his eyeballs popped out and sprang toward me.

"Arghhh!" I screamed like someone in a horror movie. But I wasn't acting.

"Ha! Fooled you," Eddie said.

"How'd you do it?" I asked when my heart rate had slowed down enough for me to speak.

Eddie showed me the trick. He had a black mask and had treated some pop-out-eyeball glasses with glow-in-the-dark paint. When he shone his flashlight on his face for twenty seconds, his eyeballs glowed for another twenty. He looked pretty freakish.

Other Trick-or-Treaters Out That Night

- 37 witches
- a trio dressed as the Lion, the Witch, and the Wardrobe
- 5 Vikings
- 12 vampires/Draculas with better costumes than mine
- 2 Wonder Women and 3 Supergirls — all adults
- 2 Batmen — father and son
- 1 Frankenstein
- 13 ghosts (not counting Gordon) wearing sheets with holes for eyes
- 16 zombies
- 1 Justin Bieber look-alike followed by 9 screaming girls
- 6 pirates, but only one had a parrot
- 2 police officers — they might have been real

Most of the people wandering the streets were little kids who should have been in bed already, out with their moms and dads. The little monsters kept mistaking us for adults.

"Twick or tweat?" a little girl with a pink tutu and a witch's hat asked Eddie. She already had a plastic cauldron stuffed with candy. We had nothing to give away, so Eddie went with the trick option. He turned away, shone the flashlight in his face, and lurched at the ballerina witch. His glow-in-the-dark eyes flew out from his hood and knocked her hat off her head.

She dropped her cauldron and started bawling.

"What do you think you're doing, scaring a little girl like that?" A woman with green skin and purple string hair came running over to us, waving her broomstick. "Go away, you brutes, ruining it for the little ones."

"It's *trick* or treat, right?" Eddie said, but the witch mother was stuffing a chocolate spider into the baby witch's mouth and ignored him.

The first house we came to was decorated with pumpkins and sparkly bats in the windows. We rang the bell.

An old lady wearing ripped pink tights, a silver minidress, and a tiara opened the door. She waved a silver wand topped with a glittering star.

"Entertain me," she said. "Come on, earn your treat." She waved the wand at us again and twirled around. "Sing! Dance! I used to be a chorus girl, you know."

She expected us to perform to earn our candy? This wasn't part of the mission plan.

Luckily, the ghost with no eyes was ready. Gordon's voice piped up from under his sheet. "We wish you a

merry Christmas. We wish you a merry Christmas."

Eddie and I joined in with a gruff "We wish you a merry Chriss-muss — And a happy new year."

"Hopeless. The wrong season and everything," the old lady said. "Now let me inspect your costumes."

She tapped each of us in turn with her wand, and like idiots we each stomped around in a circle. I never knew Halloween could be so humiliating, but we had to raise the money for the flight to Russia somehow.

"Nice mask but no effort anywhere else," she said to Eddie, and handed him one sourball.

"What are you supposed to be?" she asked me.

"Count Dracula."

"I didn't know vampires were so tall. You must have a massive coffin. Anyway, isn't he supposed to have a white face, not a brown streaky one? I thought you were a were-wolf. Two candies for trying." The sourballs were sticky, as if they had been in the package for five or six years.

She scrutinized Gordon. "Are you sure there's a real person under that sheet? How can he see where he's going?"

"He's blind," I said, which wasn't a total lie. When Gordon took off his glasses, he couldn't see. "We're looking after him."

"Poor thing. Here, take the rest of the package."

The sell-by date on the bag was sometime in the last millennium. We'd never be able to sell them.

"What did she mean, 'brown streaky face'?" I said when we were safely back on the sidewalk.

"You've got a brown streaky face." Eddie nodded and his eyes flopped toward me, bouncing up and down on their springs.

I ducked down and looked at myself in a car's side mirror. Sure enough, Count Dracula looked like he'd been under a sunlamp for hours.

"I can't understand it. The stuff was white when it came out of the tube."

"What was it called on the outside?" Gordon asked.

"Instant Copper something," I said.

"Fake tan," Eddie said. "Goes on white, skin turns brown later. You can always borrow Gordon's sheet for school tomorrow if it doesn't come off."

"What do you mean? I don't want to be a vampire with a streaky werewolf face forever. I'm an alien."

"They won't mind on Kepler 22b," the ghost with no eyes said. "They'll think it's an Earth thing."

He was right. The rest of my species on Kepler 22b would be so pleased to see me, they wouldn't care what I looked like. The kids at school wouldn't be so sympathetic.

"Dad has something in stock called Miracle Stain Removing Cream," Eddie said. "It's supposed to be for cleaning ovens, but I'm sure it'll do the trick."

If Eddie really thought I was going to plaster my face with skin-eating cream, he was wrong. I was stuck with a brown streaky face forever.

"Let's get a move on," I said. The sooner I was on my way to Kepler 22b, the better.

The people at the next few houses didn't comment on our costumes. They just gave us a few candies.

"One point six seven." Gordon's voice was more muffled than usual because of the sheet. "That's how many pieces of candy we're averaging, one point six seven per house. It's going to take us a long time to get enough for the candy store."

He was right. My shopping bag contained two gummy snakes (small ones), six cola bottles, and three oranges. Oranges! Who gave oranges at Halloween?

"We can't give up yet," I said. "How much do you think we can sell this stuff for?"

"Fifty cents. Seventy-five on a good day," the muffled voice answered.

No way was that enough to get me to Russia.

The lights were off at the next house, and there was no carved pumpkin on the step. Eddie rang the bell anyway.

"Trick or treat," he said in an upbeat voice when the door opened.

The man didn't need to dress up in a costume. His own white hair and matching bushy eyebrows made him look like a nutty professor.

"Wait here," he said.

He went away and returned with a huge bucket. Things were looking up.

"Trick!" he shouted as he chucked a bucketful of water over us. "That'll teach you. Spongers!" He slammed the door in our faces.

"That's it. I'm going home." Gordon pulled the sopping sheet from his head and threw it on the ground. "I'm not helping you anymore." He tilted his laptop, and water trickled onto the sidewalk.

"It'll dry out," I said.

Gordon the Geek, my second-best friend, flipped me off and left.

# 17

## A Spark of Genius

Okay, I admit it, the trick-or-treating thing was a waste of time. The grand total of our fundraising efforts was two gummy snakes. Eddie ate the cola bottles. I gave the oranges to Mom.

Luckily, Gordon's laptop did dry out. Otherwise I'd have lost my second-best friend and might have been stuck on Earth forever.

Jessie's high school was hosting a bonfire with fireworks. I didn't want to go. Looking up at the night sky, knowing my real home and family were out there, would just depress me. I managed to persuade Mom to let me stay inside because of the hypothermia. Amazingly, she said I could invite Eddie and Gordon over to keep me company.

We were in my room. Eddie wanted to see the fireworks, so we turned off all the lights and opened the curtains. My two best friends lazed on the floor watching the pyrotechnics while I lay on my bed looking at the ceiling and thinking how far away Kepler 22b seemed now.

"Aren't you supposed to be exercising?" Eddie asked as he stared out the window. "You know, getting fit to be an astronaut?"

"What's the point?" I said. "No money. No chance of joining any space program. No Kepler 22b."

"Have you ever seen *ET*?" Gordon's voice came out of the shadows. His laptop was closed. Eddie said the light would ruin the fireworks show. There was a streetlight right outside my window, so it wasn't pitch-black anyway.

"*ET* is for kids," I said.

"Yeah, but did you see it when you were a kid?"

"Sure."

*Bang!*

"That was a good one." Eddie pointed out the window as rockets exploded overhead.

"ET was abandoned on Earth," Gordon said. "He was an alien kid like you."

"He wasn't like me. He could hardly speak, and he was bald, and he was very short even though he had a long neck. Tell him, Eddie. I am not ET."

"Woo-hoo!" Eddie said to the fireworks outside.

"ET didn't have to go anywhere to join the space program," Gordon said. "He called up his mom and dad to come and get him."

There was a weighty pause in the room. You could almost see it, but the lights were out.

I sat up in bed. "Are you suggesting we try to phone Kepler 22b?" Maybe it was time to promote Gordon the Geek to first-best friend.

"They might not realize they left you behind. Or maybe they think you're happy with your human family after all this time."

"Maybe you aren't an alien after all." Eddie pushed his

face up against the window, smearing the glass with nose grease. He licked his finger and added some spit. "This is an alien." He pointed to the smear on the glass, which could have been a picture. It had two heads.

"Shut up, Eddie! Gordon, I've said it before and I'll say it again. *You are a genius.* How do I phone home?"

# 18

## The Supreme Communications Device

Eddie and Gordon drove me nuts sometimes, but they were the best friends an alien misfit like me could ever have hoped for.

It took him a week, but this time Gordon truly outdid himself.

"Behold! The Supreme Communications Device!" Gordon said as he opened his briefcase.

"What's that?" Eddie stabbed a greasy potato-chip–flavored finger at a USB port stuck in the middle.

Gordon snatched the circuit board away. "I constructed this in a static-free environment."

Eddie licked his finger. "It's okay, Gordon. Cheese and onion today. They were out of static."

Gordon moved his device out of Eddie's reach.

"I am missing two vital components. A keyboard and a communications satellite."

"We can use your laptop," I said. "That's a keyboard."

"No we can*not*," Gordon said.

That's when I realized Gordon was my *second*-best friend for a reason. He wasn't prepared to sacrifice his laptop for the mission.

"Okay, so where can we get a keyboard?" I asked.

"Leave that to me," Eddie said.

Eddie was the best friend an alien could have. He always delivered. No doubt his dad had received a shipment of laptops.

With Eddie supplying the keyboard and Gordon building the communications device, it was only fair for me to provide the satellite.

"When you say 'satellite,' what exactly do you mean?" I asked Gordon the Geek.

Gordon took off his glasses and cleaned them on the end of his necktie.

When he took his glasses off, I was amazed at how small his eyes looked without them. His head was probably small too. Maybe Gordon was small because he saved his lunch money instead of buying lunch with it. *He'll never grow as tall as me if he doesn't eat,* I thought. And then I remembered, he'd never grow as tall as me, because he was human.

"Any kind of satellite dish should work." Gordon put his glasses back on. "I'll have to reverse the polarity to make it transmit rather than receive. It should be able to relay back to the central satellite and then to any other communications devices up there."

He pointed at the ceiling light, although I think he meant the satellites up in space. "So long as someone from Kepler 22b is monitoring our communications, they should hear us."

"Someone?" Eddie said. "Don't you mean some*thing?* Maybe Keplerites have a hundred tentacles and acid for blood."

"You've been watching too many movies." I glared at Eddie. Just when things were getting serious, he had to get all silly again. "I am *an* alien, not *the* Alien."

"Are you sure?" Eddie grinned. "Should I look under your bed to see if you're incubating eggs or something?"

There are times when I want to grind Eddie's face into the carpet.

So how come he's my best friend?

The backstory is, we started at daycare on the same day. While I sat on the rug listening to a story with the other kids, Eddie ran around us in circles, pushing a toy vacuum cleaner and shouting, "To 'finity and behind!" I thought he was pretty cool. The next day, I ran in circles with him and never listened at story time again. We've been best friends ever since.

Until now.

He wasn't interested in helping me.

I had to show my total commitment to this project, even if it meant upsetting my human family.

"I have a satellite," I said.

# 19

## The Trouble with Satellites

I knew my human family would be upset when they found out I had removed their only way to watch TV. But when they realized I'd taken the satellite dish to further my mission to relocate myself to Kepler 22b, they'd have to forgive me. I'm not really one of the family, after all, and they'd be happy to see me go.

Why My Family Would Be Glad I'd Left Earth

1. Timmy could have my room. It was much bigger than his bedroom, and he'd be able to lay out all of my old wooden railway and build a Duplo city around it using every single brick, just like I used to do. He'd love it.

2. Jessie has always said she wished I'd never

existed, so she'd be thrilled that I was out of her life.

3.  Mom would no longer have to carry giant packages of single-serving boxes of Mega Flakes from the supermarket. She'd have more space on the top shelf for stuff like rice/pasta/beans. She wouldn't be able to reach them, but she could always buy a stepladder that didn't answer back.

4.  Dad would be happy to stop getting a crick in his neck from looking up at me when he told me off. He'd never have to visit the chiropractor again.

I was pretty sure my family would agree that one measly satellite dish was a fair price to pay to be rid of me. But I hadn't left Earth yet, and there might be a delay before my alien family came for me. I was a little worried about what my human family might do to me during that time.

The only problem with satellite dishes is they tend to be attached to a vertical wall quite high up on the front of a house. Luckily, Eddie's dad had a couple of fantastic window-cleaner ladders.

Do you know how high a two-story house is? About thirty feet. That's high.

Eddie's dad's long, narrow ladder looked pretty flimsy propped up against the front wall of our house.

"That's high," I said, looking up at the satellite dish.

"That's high," Eddie said.

Fully extended, the ladder reached the skinny section of wall between the satellite dish and my parents' bedroom window. To remove the dish, I'd have to climb to the very top of the ladder and duck behind the dish to reach the screws.

One side of our house is attached to the house next door. On the other side (the satellite side), our house isn't attached to anything. There's a dark alley, a fence, another dark alley, then the wall of Mrs. Fagan's house. That dark chasm of doom between the houses made the ladder look even flimsier.

I would have been perfectly happy to stand around saying "That's high" all day if it meant I didn't have to climb that ladder.

"Up you go, then," Eddie said.

"I thought you were here to help me," I said.

"I supplied the ladder."

"I'm supplying the satellite dish."

"Not unless you get it off the wall," Eddie said.

He was right, of course. Without that satellite dish, I'd remain exiled on Earth forever.

I had no choice.

I put my foot on the bottom rung of the ladder. It was rock solid.

"You aren't scared, are you?" Eddie asked.

"If I fall, will you catch me?" I said, changing the subject.

"No. But I'll make sure your ashes are shipped to Russia so an astronaut can scatter them in space."

*That's* a best friend.

I gripped the ladder with both hands and climbed.

Do you know what *vertigo* means? Look it up in the dictionary. It's an impressive word and will earn you extra credit in English if you use it. I found out all about it on that ladder.

A wave of fear burst from my Keplerite psyche and slammed my alien body against the ladder. My right cheek pressed so hard against the rungs that I could feel the ridged imprint of the tread being tattooed on my face. My eyes stared unblinking at the ground below me.

The ladder and I were Super Glued together. The dark chasm of doom loomed large between my house and Mrs. Fagan's. Any minute it was going to leap up and swallow me whole.

"You okay, Dan?" Eddie called up to me.

I couldn't answer. Even my tongue was paralyzed. I gripped the sides of the ladder and willed it to crash to the ground just to get it over with.

"Dan?" Eddie's voice seemed small coming from way down there on the sidewalk. I pressed my cheek farther into the ladder and closed my eyes.

"Dan!" Eddie's voice was right by my ear now. "Let

go." A greasy, potato-chip-scented hand yanked my fingers away from the ladder.

I couldn't open my eyes. I didn't want to see my best friend hanging precariously from the ladder over the chasm of doom. The same ladder that my poor, terrified Keplerite body was stuck to.

"I've got you," Eddie said. "One step down."

He nudged my left foot, and somehow I plucked up the courage to move it down one rung.

"Now the other foot," he said.

My other foot came down.

"Okay, two more steps."

I managed to move each foot twice more, and then—miraculously—I was standing on the ground. My legs felt like two rubber bands.

"It's high up there," I said.

"How would you know? You only made it to the fourth rung."

The downstairs window opened next door.

"Are you doing windows now, Daniel?" Mrs. Fagan called. "I'll give you five dollars if you clean mine, front and back."

Five dollars was more than we'd made from our

Halloween money-making scheme, which was none, but I'd have to get farther than the fourth rung of the ladder to do a really good job. So I turned her down and tried not to think too much about the crisp green five-dollar bill that could have been mine.

"Catch me if I fall," Eddie said with a grin. He sprinted up the ladder like a squirrel up a tree. Two minutes later he was back on the ground with the satellite dish.

# 20

## Hiding the Evidence

When something is at the top of a two-story house, it looks pretty small. When it's down on the ground, right next to you on the sidewalk, it's much bigger.

The satellite dish was *huge*.

I had no idea how Eddie had managed to disconnect my family's satellite TV and get the dish down the ladder so quickly. Maybe his dad had been in the satellite business before he became a store owner.

"You stash this." Eddie leaned the huge dish against the wall. "I'll go get the keyboard." And he was gone.

I didn't hang around, because

1. If the police drove past, they'd probably arrest me, and that would be the end of my return to Kepler 22b. If those Keplerites

knew I had a criminal record, they probably wouldn't come and get me.

2. If Mom came home, the mission would be over for a completely different reason. She'd kill me for removing the dish. And once she'd finished killing me, she'd hand me over to Dad for more of the same. When I'd been well and truly murdered by my human parents, Jessie would take over.

It was essential that my family not discover who had stolen the satellite dish.

I needed to find the perfect hiding place.

Luckily, there was a dark chasm of doom handy. I hid the dish in the alley between Mrs. Fagan's house and ours.

That left the ladder.

When Eddie brought the ladder over, it was a lot shorter. Somehow it had been collapsed down and stacked in more manageable lengths. Fully extended, a thirty-foot ladder is a tricky customer. I didn't know how to unextend it, and I was running out of time. Mom was due back from work any minute.

I figured the chasm of doom was big enough to

swallow the ladder whole. I grabbed the ladder away from the house, meaning to lower it smoothly to the ground.

But the ladder had other ideas. First it tottered left. Then it swung around to the right. Thirty feet of untamed ladder reared above me like a giant cobra, its head bobbing here and there, looking for a place to strike.

Then it found the perfect target: Mrs. Fagan's brand-new car. The ladder twirled around on one leg and went into free fall. I shut my eyes and waited for the crash.

Silence.

I opened my eyes, thinking maybe the cobra had decided to take me out instead and I was now unconscious.

But no. My hands were still holding the ladder. It was stuck at a forty-five-degree angle to the ground.

The head of the ladder had entwined itself in a wire running between our house and a telegraph pole farther down the street.

The snake was tamed.

I studied the angle between the ladder and the ground and gave the ladder a yank. At last the ladder crashed down into the chasm of doom. Right where I needed it.

Success!

I had no idea why there had been a wire leading to the corner of our house, but it wasn't there now. One end was still connected to the telegraph pole, and the other end lay dead on the pavement. It wasn't spitting sparks or anything, so I figured it wasn't important.

*What is a telegraph pole, anyway?* I wondered. Something to do with Morse code and telegrams. The members of my human family were more sophisticated than that. They used the telephone and email to keep in touch. Dad would most likely be delighted to be rid of that random wire.

The mission now owned a satellite dish. With Eddie's keyboard and Gordon's communications device, I was about to be reunited with my real family on Kepler 22b. I couldn't wait.

I had just gone back into the house when Jessie came home from school, Random Mood Generator on Obnoxious.

"Don't mess with me, Beanpole," she said as she pushed past me. "I'm getting together with my friends in a mega virtual hangout. We're going to annihilate Serena Blake!"

She rushed into the family room and turned on the computer. Then she poked her head out and said, "Do not disturb. Get it?"

She slammed the family room door.

Every evening it's the same old Do Not Disturb routine. I've never disturbed her boring virtual hangout, and I didn't care what she did to Serena Blake. I had much more important communications to tackle before bedtime. I went up to my room to wait for Eddie and Gordon.

"Arghh!" Jessie screamed, so loudly I could hear it

through my tightly closed bedroom door. I wondered if she was being murdered, but I figured it was none of my business.

My door flew open, and Jessie burst into my room, Random Mood Generator stuck on Murderous.

"Have you been messing with the computer?" she said.

"No," I said.

"There's no Internet service."

"Nothing to do with me."

"Arghhh!" she screamed.

Then I heard the key in the front door.

"Mom's home," I said.

"You are the most annoying brother *ever*, and I wish you'd never been born!" Jessie yelled. She slammed my door and charged downstairs.

"I wasn't born, I was dumped, remember?" I shouted after her, but she didn't answer.

I suppose I was born on Kepler 22b. Or maybe on the journey to Earth.

There was a whole lot about life in the Kepler 22b world that I knew nothing about. But I did know a whole lot about life on Earth. And Jessie the Random Mood Queen was one thing I wouldn't miss when I was back with my alien family.

# **21**

# **The Weird Case of the Hypnotic Laptop**

Jessie was still screaming. I didn't know why humans had to be so loud. My alien ears were very sensitive.

I plugged in my headphones and buried my head under my pillow. I might have suffocated if Eddie hadn't pulled the pillow off my face. Gordon was already in the corner tapping away on his laptop.

"Your sister's going crazy downstairs," Eddie said.

"She *is* crazy. Have you got the keyboard?"

Eddie plunked a cardboard box on my bed.

It wasn't any old box—it was the original packaging for a brand-new laptop. And the brand-new laptop was still in the box.

Normally, Gordon doesn't say much. He sits in the background stupefied by his own brainpower. Except when there's a brand-new laptop in the room.

Gordon fell on the box, ripped it open, and started

sniffing the foam packing material as if it was infused with perfume.

"It's a Microcron Airweight 587X.SDR." Gordon's voice had slipped into a weird monotone as if someone had hypnotized him. I didn't know what was in that foam, but it was having a bizarre effect on him.

"Dad got a job lot. He's selling them cheap," Eddie said. "Something about the case not being quite up to standard."

As you know, I'm not very technically minded, but even I was impressed with that laptop. It was no thicker than a thin-crust pizza, and the cool midnight-blue case looked perfect to me.

Gordon stroked the thin-crust laptop and sighed as he lifted the lid to reveal the keyboard. A silly smile spread across his face.

Did I mention that I always wanted a computer of my own? I was already thinking that maybe the thin-crust laptop was too nice to use for a communications device. Maybe it would be more suitable for going back to Kepler 22b with me. It was small enough to fit in my backpack, and I'd probably be able to persuade Eddie to give it to me as a goodbye present. But Gordon had his own agenda. He whispered nonsense syllables and giggled as he tiptoed his fingers over the keys. He was flirting with the laptop. *My* laptop.

I reached out and placed my palm firmly on the midnight-blue lid.

Gordon snatched the laptop away and snapped it shut.

"It isn't suitable for my device," he said. His voice had gone all high and wobbly. I had heard him speak like that once before, when Mr. Pitdown accused him of using the Internet to do research about the Egyptians instead of using a book like we were supposed to. Gordon had been lying then, and I suspected he was lying now.

"What do you mean?" I said. "It's a keyboard, isn't it?"

"The wrong type of keyboard." Gordon fixed his eyes on me. Magnified by the thick lenses of his glasses, his eyeballs bulged out of their sockets.

I'd never had a staring contest with Gordon before. Normally his eyes are focused on his laptop screen, not staring me down like a demon. It was terrifying. I didn't want to be ripped to shreds by Gordon the Demon, but I still needed to phone my relatives on Kepler 22b and ask them to come and get me.

"What about the communications device?" I whispered without blinking.

"We'll use *my* laptop." Gordon pushed his glasses back up his nose but didn't take his demon eyes off me.

"You mean the laptop you said we couldn't use?"

"I'm prepared to make the sacrifice. I just need to transfer my stuff to this one."

The Geek's eyelids must have been Super Glued open. He didn't blink once. During this mission I'd had my doubts about the level of commitment of my two best friends, but suddenly Gordon was serious. Deadly serious. I knew the mission was at an end if Gordon didn't get to keep the thin-crust laptop.

But it was Eddie's dad's laptop. What if Eddie said no?

Do you know what tension looks like? Me neither. But I felt it in the room right then. It was an invisible seething mass of darkness with crackles of electricity at the edges.

Gordon wanted the thin-crust laptop.

I wanted to get to Kepler 22b.

I stared into those demon eyes for what felt like an hour. I didn't know which I was more afraid of, being stranded here on Earth or being stranded here on Earth with Gordon. In the end I decided Gordon could have the stupid laptop. I blinked and the staring match was over.

Gordon turned his bulbous eyes on Eddie.

Eddie's lousy at staring contests. He tends to get bored and smash his opponent right between the eyes. That's cheating, of course, but his opponent is normally too busy nursing a bruised face to argue. But normally there isn't a laptop at stake.

Gordon stared at Eddie.

Eddie stared at Gordon.

No one blinked.

I willed Gordon's eyeballs to stay in their sockets.

I willed Eddie's hands to stay at his sides.

The tension grew darker, more dangerous.

After a couple of zillion years, Eddie spoke.

"Whatever!" he said, and looked away. "There's plenty more where that came from."

Gordon the Geek pulled his eyeballs in, and the tension fizzled to almost nothing.

When tension disappears, it leaves a huge "What was that all about?" black hole.

The mission and our friendship had nearly been destroyed.

Gordon fumbled in his briefcase for a bunch of cables and connected the two laptops together as if everything was business as usual.

I raised an eyebrow at Eddie. He raised both eyebrows in return. He can't do the one-eyebrow thing, but it was good to share solidarity eyebrows with someone.

I was going to miss him when I was gone. I wasn't sure I'd miss Gordon.

"The data transfer will take another seven minutes and fifty-six seconds," Gordon said in a normal voice, as if he hadn't just reverted from being a bulging-eyed demon. "Where is the satellite? I have to figure out how to reverse the polarity before I connect it."

It felt good to get out of my bedroom. I left the door open, hoping that the last shadow of tension would be gone by the time we got back. I led the way downstairs, ignoring the screaming coming from the kitchen, and out to the chasm of doom. The chasm was even darker than normal, but I could just make out the silver satellite dish in the gloom.

"That's no good," Gordon said. "A satellite dish has to be up high if it's going to work. You know, near the roof or something."

"Now you tell us," Eddie said.

I couldn't speak because my teeth were gnashing together uncontrollably. I'd faced death on that ladder for nothing.

"That would be the perfect spot." Gordon pointed to the skinny section of wall outside my parents' bedroom.

I still couldn't speak. I turned to Eddie and raised my eyebrow again. This time the eyebrow quivered wildly.

"Okay," he said. "But you owe me."

Eddie might have a few disgusting personal habits, but he is the best friend anyone could wish for.

# 22

# Communication — How to Do It

Jessie's wailing filled the whole house. Gordon and I crept past the kitchen door.

"I can't get it to work." Mom sounded frazzled. "Call the phone company."

"I could help them," Gordon whispered.

"No! Not till we've sent our message to Kepler 22b."

We were halfway up the stairs when Jessie screamed again. "The phone's dead!"

"The phone and Internet come in on the same wire," Mom said. "Pass me my cell phone."

Maybe that random wire lying dead on the sidewalk wasn't so random after all. I didn't hang around to hear the rest of the conversation. I ushered Gordon upstairs, and it wasn't long before Eddie joined us.

"Satellite dish in position," he said. "Ladder out of sight."

I gave Eddie a thumbs-up.

When Gordon is being geeky rather than freaky, he is very professional. It took him two minutes to connect his old laptop and the satellite dish (via a very long cable) to his communications device.

"What message do you want to send?" he asked.

My mind did what it always does when I'm asked a question under pressure. It turned stark-white empty.

"Well, Mr. Kendal?" Gordon put on his bored tone.

"S.O.S.?" I suggested.

"Are you in danger?"

"Not right now, but Jessie hasn't tried to turn on the TV yet."

"How about . . ." Gordon started typing. *Kepler 22b. Alien waiting for transfer. Please collect me from 26 Beechwood Road.* He looked over at me and raised his eyebrows above the frames of his glasses.

A few minutes earlier he was going to kill me, but now he gave me the solidarity eyebrows. He pointed at the Enter key and waggled his eyebrows at me.

For the first time ever, Gordon was inviting me to touch his laptop. Maybe he felt guilty about the whole demon-eyeball thing, or maybe he didn't care about his old keyboard now that he'd moved on to the thin-crust laptop.

I rubbed my finger clean on my jeans and pressed the Enter key.

The laptop screen sprang into life. Streams of writing scrolled up and off the screen. As the words sped past, I could see they were in foreign languages. There were accents and weird letters all over the place.

Kepler 22b. Extranjero de espera para la transferencia. Por favor, me recoger a partir del 26 Carretera Beechwood

Kepler 22b. Alien čekání na přenos. Prosím, sbírat mě z 26 Road Beechwood.

কপেলার 22b. স্থানান্তর এলিয়েন জন্য অপেক্ষা করছে. 26 Beechwood রো·ড থেকে সম্পর্কে সংগ্রহ দয়া করে.

Kepler 22b. Alien bíða flutnings. Vinsamlegast safna mér úr 26 Beechwood Road.

ケプラー22bは。エイリアン転送待ち。 26ぶなの道から私を収集してください

"What's happening? Where did my message go?"

"Out there." Gordon pointed through the window at the starlit sky. "In every language known to man. German, Tagalog, Cantonese. I put your message through

133

a universal translator. Once it's done the languages, it will move on to Morse code, semaphore, and pictograms."

"Gordon, you're a genius!" I wanted to kiss him, but with his hang-ups I didn't dare risk it. I gave him a thumbs-up instead.

My message streamed up the laptop screen in languages I didn't recognize. He'd even translated it into Egyptian hieroglyphs.

"Bean?" Dad called up the stairs. "Can you come down here a minute?"

His voice seemed to come from a different world. A world I no longer belonged to.

"Daniel Kendal!" As soon as he said my real name, I knew he was serious. I didn't want to leave the Supreme Communications Device, but if Dad came upstairs, he'd want to know why a cable was going into the front bedroom.

"Keep communicating as long as possible," I said to Gordon and Eddie, then dashed downstairs to face my human family.

"Do you have anything upstairs that might be . . . well, shady?" Dad said. He had a lot of worry lines across his forehead. "I know Eddie says his dad's business is strictly legit, but I want to double-check."

I didn't know whether communicating with an alien species was questionable, but even if it was, I wasn't going to tell Dad about it.

"No," I said.

"Has Ed brought anything over that might be stolen?"

Did he mean the thin-crust laptop?

"Because I've called the police, and I don't want to get Ed into trouble."

"The police?" I said in my most innocent voice.

"Some idiots stole our satellite dish and pulled down the telephone wire while they were at it. We have no TV, no phone, and no Internet. All communications are cut off, except for cell phones."

That wasn't strictly true.

Normally Dad would have been impressed by Gordon's invention, but I couldn't share it with him right now. I'd tell him all about it when it was time to say goodbye.

Suddenly I felt a thick lump in my throat. When I blasted off for Kepler 22b, I'd leave everything behind. Everything and everyone.

"Dad, something's happening!" Jessie yelled.

We went into the family room. Jessie was standing in front of the TV with a remote control in each hand, zapping them furiously in turn.

"I had something just now," she said as she zapped.

The TV screen buzzed with black-and-white fuzziness. Then it cleared, and a stream of writing scrolled up endlessly. A stream of writing in every language on Earth.

"I think you should turn it off." I jumped in front of the screen. I wasn't sure how good Jessie was at languages. She might recognize "Beechwood Road" in Afrikaans.

"Get out of the way!" She shoved me just as the last line of foreign language disappeared off the top of the screen.

The TV started bleeping.

-.- ..---.. -. . . . . -. / ..--- -..--- - ---. . .

That sort of thing.

"Sounds like Morse code," Dad said.

"Turn it off! Turn it off! It's going to explode!" I reached for the power button. In the moment before the screen blacked out, a picture flashed onto the screen.

A live picture of a geeky kid with thick glasses peering into a computer screen.

Gordon the Geek had left his webcam on.

# 23

## Too Close for Comfort

"What was that?" Jessie kept zapping the remotes.

"Just static," I said.

"It wasn't static. It looked like a person."

"You're hallucinating," I said. "You've got your friends on the brain, so you imagined seeing them on the screen."

"I don't have any friends who look like that. But *you* do." She jabbed my chest with a remote control.

"Kids, kids. Please. We're all having a bad day. Don't take it out on each other." Dad took the remotes out of Jessie's hands. "There's clearly a problem here, so let's calm down and find something else to do."

"But, Dad—" Jessie began.

"But nothing," Dad said.

Jessie didn't say anything. She narrowed her eyes at me and set her Random Mood Generator to Psycho.

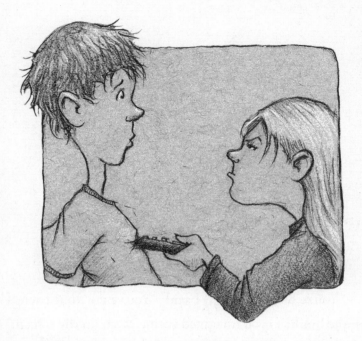

"I thought you said the satellite dish was missing." Mom came into the room, her hands on her hips, tiredness on her face.

"It is," Dad said.

"Not anymore," Mom said.

While Dad and Jessie followed her out the front door, I raced upstairs.

"They're onto us. Disconnect, quickly," I said to my two friends, who sat mesmerized by the message scrolling up the screen on a continuous loop.

Gordon pulled out the wires and shoved his circuit board under the bed.

"I'm telling you, it wasn't there before." Dad's voice came from the downstairs hallway.

"Well, it's there now." Mom closed the front door. "And Timmy's playhouse has been trashed. We'll have to put it back together in the morning."

Eddie and I dashed into my parents' bedroom. Eddie reached out the window and replaced Gordon's cable with the disconnected TV cable.

The message had been sent and the components of Gordon's communications device were separated. TV would be restored downstairs, I hoped. The only problem was the dead phone wire. I couldn't do anything about that. I was sorry, but sometimes there are casualties on a mission.

"Dad says the police are on their way," I said. "That laptop isn't stolen, is it?"

"No!" Eddie said. "At least I don't think so." He tried to grab the thin-crust laptop, but Gordon got to it first.

"Mine!" Gordon said.

Eddie didn't argue.

"Okay by me, Gordon my friend. I'm out of here just

in case. Dad says it's best not to be on first-name terms with the police."

The doorbell rang.

Eddie threw open the window and was shinning down the drainpipe before I could stop him.

"Are you leaving that way too?" I asked Gordon.

"I prefer to use the door," he said.

"What about the police?"

"I haven't done anything wrong."

"What about the laptop?"

"Eddie says it isn't stolen." Gordon shrugged. "And they're looking for a satellite dish, anyway."

I went downstairs with him, just in case the police didn't see it his way.

# 24

## The Chosen One

I took a deep breath and opened the door, expecting to be arrested immediately. But it wasn't the police.

It was a crowd of weird-looking strangers.

"That's him!" A woman with frizzy vermilion hair and long, shabby clothes pointed at Gordon. "Take me with you!" She threw herself at our feet.

Gordon edged backward as the woman pawed at his sneakers.

"What are you talking about?" I said.

"Kepler 22b. Take me with you." The woman clasped her hands together as if in prayer. "I beg you!"

"Seems like the message worked," Gordon said.

I wasn't so sure. It was clear the message had gone somewhere. But had it reached Kepler 22b? The woman lying on our path didn't look like a Keplerite to me.

"That's him! That's him!" Two more weirdos ran

toward us. One had stringy gray hair and a long gray beard. His hair was so long that the ends of it had been knitted into his droopy sweater. A small woman skipped by his side. She wore a faded patchwork skirt and strings of brightly colored beads around her neck.

"Get up, Myrtle," the man said to the horizontal woman. "Move aside so we can get closer to our savior."

Whatever result I expected from sending the message to Kepler 22b, this wasn't it. These people couldn't be aliens. For starters, they were too short. And if they had been adult Keplerites, surely they would have figured out how to get back to Kepler 22b on their own.

"I think there's some mistake," I said.

"No mistake! No mistake!" the patchwork woman singsonged. "This *is* 26 Beechwood Road, isn't it?" She skipped forward and twirled around so that her beads swung out in all directions. She made me feel dizzy.

Just to be sure, I asked, "Are you an alien?"

"No, no, no!" The woman clasped her hands to her mouth and crouched down in a huddle of quivering patchwork. "I'm not worthy," she said.

"We are the Returned," the man announced. He opened his arms wide and looked up at the night sky. "The superior species returned us to Earth."

"Heavens forgive us. We were not worthy," Horizontal Myrtle said, tears in her eyes.

"I think we've got a case of alien abductees," Gordon said, trying not to move his lips.

I thought we had a case of wackos.

"I don't get it," I said out of the corner of my mouth.

"They were abducted by aliens and then returned. Or think they were," Gordon said. "They must have picked up our message, and now they want to go back to Kepler 22b with you."

No way! The Keplerites or some other alien species had rejected them. If they came with me, I might get mistaken for a Returner and be rejected as well.

A silver RV pulled up on the other side of the road. It had blacked-out windows and a satellite dish on the roof.

Beardie Sweater and Patchwork Woman snapped out of their dreamy trance.

"It's the others!" Patchwork Woman gasped.

"Quick, Myrtle!" Beardie Sweater shouted. "The others mustn't get credit for finding the first alien on Earth. Grab him!"

Horizontal Myrtle lunged forward, her purple fingernails as sharp as talons.

"But I'm not an alien," Gordon protested, cowering.

"We *saw* you," Myrtle hissed. "And so did the superior species. When they arrive, we will be waiting with you."

"You've got the wrong kid," Gordon said, fixing his terrified eyes on me. The problem with phobias is they trump every other human emotion, and Gordon didn't want these hairy weirdos to touch him. I knew what he was going to say next. *"He's the —"*

I clapped my hand over his mouth, dragged him back into the house, and slammed the door on Myrtle's hissing face.

# 25

## When Is a Friend Not a Friend?

"What did you do that for?" I shouted.

Gordon pulled out a disinfectant wipe and swiped it over his mouth.

"I didn't know what else to do," he said.

"You were going to hand me over to those maniacs!" I said.

"They want to go to Kepler 22b with you."

"Do you really think *I* want to go to Kepler 22b with *them*?"

The doorbell rang again.

"Are you going home or what?" I said. "I think your friends are waiting for you outside. Maybe you'll get home alive."

"They are *not* my friends," he said. "Anyway, they want the real alien. They want you."

"No!" I stabbed Gordon in the chest with an angry

alien finger. "They want the four-eyed geek who beamed his image across the airwaves along with my serious message."

"Don't touch me!" Gordon clutched his briefcase to his chest as he shrank away from me. "I just want to go home and install my software."

Typical! Gordon didn't care if those nutcases ripped me apart as long as no one touched *him*. He didn't care about anything except his crazy hang-ups and getting it on with his thin-crust laptop.

Mom and Dad appeared in the hallway.

"Excuse me, boys. That'll be the police," Dad said.

"Go in the kitchen and find something to eat," Mom said. "Then I'll drive you home, Gordon. Those satellite thieves might still be in the area."

Mom didn't have a clue that the real satellite thieves were in the kitchen or that we were no longer friends. I couldn't forgive Gordon for pointing me out to the weirdo Returners.

Gordon helped himself to a drink of water. He'd never drunk or eaten anything at my house before. I knew he just wanted to look at something besides me.

Jessie stormed in from the family room, her Random Mood Generator still on Psycho.

"Oh, it's you," she said to Gordon. "I saw you on TV earlier."

"I think you may be mistaken," Gordon said.

"I don't think so. But it wasn't on any regular TV channel."

"Is the TV working now?" I pushed my way between my incredibly annoying sister and my former second-best friend, in case the traitor decided to turn me in to my family.

"Yeah, only now Timmy is watching cartoons and I've missed my soaps. Tragic, right?" Jessie flicked her hair away from her face.

"There are probably reruns," Gordon said.

"I'm not someone who catches up. I have to know what's happening right now. Get it?" Jessie waved her finger rudely in Gordon's face. "I'm going upstairs."

"You have to ask permission to watch TV upstairs." One of Mom's rules.

"I know," she said. "Where are Mom and Dad, anyway?"

"On the doorstep talking to . . . someone," I said. I was going to say the police, but if it had been them, Mom would have brought them in and given them coffee. I figured Mom and Dad were still trying to reason with the Returners, and I gulped down a huge gob of guilt.

Jessie flounced out, drama-queen style.

"Daniel!" she shouted two seconds later. "Get out here. Quick!"

For once, the panic in her voice sounded real, and as soon as I got into the hallway, I realized why.

The front door was wide open. Mom and Dad were gone.

# 26

# The Weird Case of the Missing Parents

How would you feel if your mom and dad disappeared two minutes after you had slammed the door on a crazed gang of alien abductees?

Those maniacs wanted aliens. I didn't know what they were going to do when they discovered that Mom and Dad were human, but I knew it would be really bad.

I felt totally sick. I ran out into the street, hoping Mom and Dad were having a chat with Mrs. Fagan next door. I didn't care if Mrs. Fagan told them I'd been messing with the ladder and had brought down the telephone wire. *Anything* was better than Mom and Dad being mistaken for aliens by the Returners. But there was no sign of Mom and Dad anywhere.

A muffled cry came from the RV parked opposite. It sounded like Mom's voice.

"Hey!" I started across the street, but the silver RV with

sinister blacked-out windows pulled away and sped off.

"Mom! Dad!" I yelled, but it was too late. The RV turned the corner and disappeared.

At that moment the middle of Beechwood Road was the loneliest place in the universe. Mom and Dad had been kidnapped and it was all my fault.

A VW camper van spluttered into life behind me. Beardie Sweater was at the wheel, Horizontal Myrtle and Patchwork Woman beside him.

I jumped up onto the bumper and slammed my fists against the windshield. "Where are they?"

"Out of the way!" Horizontal Myrtle was leaning out the window. "We are in pursuit. Our so-called leaders have taken the aliens to the rendezvous."

So the Returners had leaders! They weren't a random group of nutjobs. They were organized. They had plans. And right now those plans involved two totally innocent humans: Mom and Dad.

"Where are they taking them?"

"To higher ground, nearer the heavens. To be reunited with the superior species." Horizontal Myrtle pointed a purple fingernail at the stars.

Beardie Sweater thumped the horn again, and the van started moving. I jumped out of the way before I fell off the bumper and he ran me over. The ancient vehicle putt-putted its way down the street and disappeared around the corner.

"Will someone tell me what's going on?" Jessie demanded, her hands on her hips.

"Mom and Dad have been kidnapped," I said.

"What?" she shrieked.

"By some abductees who think your parents are aliens," Gordon said.

Jessie opened her mouth to speak, but nothing came

out. Nothing at all. For the first time in Jessie's life, her Random Mood Generator was on Empty.

"We have to rescue them," I said.

"Alien abductees?" Jessie's mouth sprang into action again. "This doesn't have anything to do with Serena Blake's gang, does it? They're called the Re-something. Revisers. No, Returners."

"You know them?" I said.

"I know *her*. I told you, she's the craziest psycho in the whole tenth grade. She is absolutely convinced that she and her family were abducted by aliens last year. She lived in their spaceship for three months and then they let her and her family go. She says it was awesome up there and she wants to go back."

"Does she have a silver RV?"

"All her relatives live in RVs. They need to be ready in case they get the call from above." She pointed to the sky.

"I think they got the call," Gordon said.

"So where have they taken Mom and Dad?" Jessie asked.

"Higher ground." I shrugged. "They think they're meeting an alien spaceship."

"Park Hill Fields," Gordon said. "That's the only open space with altitude within a five-mile radius."

"I'll get my bike," I said. "Jess, you'll have to stay here with Timmy. Gordon and I will go after them."

"No way," Jessie said. "I'm not letting you anywhere near Serena Blake on your own. She will stop at nothing to get what she wants."

I was impressed. I hadn't realized she cared.

"And anyway, I want Dad back. He's supposed to be taking me and my friends to a concert next week. I'll ride Mom's bike with the child seat for Timmy. Where's your fat friend?"

"He's not fat. He just likes potato chips," I said. "He went home."

"Call him." Jessie handed me her cell phone. "We need backup."

Things were getting weirder by the second. Jessie had never even let me look at her phone before.

Two minutes later, the Rescue Mission Team was ready to go.

Me on my bike, with Gordon perched on the luggage rack. Jessie on Mom's bike, with Timmy strapped safely in the child seat. He had a Duplo model in his hands.

154

"He wouldn't leave it behind," Jessie explained. "And I don't want one of his tantrums."

"Vroom! Vroom!" Timmy said, whooshing his Duplo model through the air like an airplane.

Eddie came zipping up the street on a mini motorbike. It sounded like a wasp in a hair dryer and was so small, his knees were practically around his ears. Probably the only bike his dad had in stock.

"Where are we going?" he asked.

"Park Hill Fields," I said.

"Follow me!" he said, and buzzed off at full speed.

# 27

## *Voulez-vous un rendez-vous?*

Park Hill Fields wasn't far away, but with Gordon on the back of my bike it felt like a million miles. It wouldn't have been so bad if he'd left his briefcase behind. It weighed a ton. When we arrived, the luggage rack was bent, but all I cared about was Mom and Dad.

Park Hill Fields is exactly what it sounds like — a park on a hill with fields of grass. It's flat right at the top, where the playground and tennis courts are.

The silver RV was parked right next to the swings. Its lights flashed on and off intermittently.

.- .- .. .. . -. / .- .. -.--.. . ---.. . . . - --- - .. ---. . . / . ---.-

-- - .. -. -

"Morse code," Gordon said.

"What's it say?" I asked.

"'We're wack jobs. Come and get us,'" Eddie said.

Gordon squinted at the flashing lights.

156

"It says, 'Alien rendezvous point,'" he said.

"Mom and Dad aren't aliens," Jessie said.

"Unfortunately, the Returners don't know that," I mumbled.

A stream of campers and mobile homes clogged the road leading to the top of the hill. Crowds of strange figures swarmed across the grass.

A lot of the Returners were wearing hippie outfits like Beardie Sweater's and his friends', but some had taken much more trouble with their costumes.

One group were dressed in black with yellow sashes across their chests. They marched up the hill in an arrow formation.

Another group were dressed as characters from *Star Trek*.

"That's Spock." Eddie pointed to a guy wearing plastic pointed ears and drawn-on Vulcan eyebrows.

"It's Mr. Pitdown," Gordon said.

Sure enough, Mr. Pitdown was dressed as Mr. Spock. Spock with a mustache.

"Jerk!" Eddie and I said together, tugging at our invisible mustaches.

"How did you"—Jessie pointed at us—"get involved with *them*?" She pointed at the Returners.

"It was a mistake," I said.

"Where's Mommy?" Timmy's voice wobbled as if he was about to cry.

The enormity of what I'd done sat like a huge boulder in front of me. Mom and Dad were now held prisoner, surrounded by a mass of deluded wackos.

They *were* deluded, weren't they? Demented, mixed up, confused, crazy?

The Returners hadn't really been taken by aliens, had they?

And I guess that was when a question started forming in my own mind. *Am I really an alien?*

"I want Mommy." Timmy put his thumb in his mouth.

Poor Timmy! I reached out to hug him, but Jessie got there first and pulled him out of the child seat. Two big Timmy tears plopped onto her shoulder as she rocked him. He was only a little kid. He needed his mom.

So did I.

# 28

## Distraction Technique

"Look. Something's happening," Eddie said.

A procession with flaming torches marched across the hilltop and circled the playground. The words *burned alive* came into my mind. I didn't want to say them aloud in front of Timmy, but the human best-friend telepathy must have been strong in the air that night. Without a word, we all dumped our bikes in the bushes and ran up the hill. Jessie had to carry Timmy, whose legs were too short for speed.

We didn't need to hide or sneak around. No one was interested in us. Every other person on that hillside was looking upward.

The Returners had stuck the flaming torches in the ground at the top of the hill. Around the torches, a ring of Returners held hands and stared into the sky. We stopped by the tennis courts to catch our breath.

A powerful searchlight swept across the night sky. "Searching for the alien spaceship," I muttered.

"Where do you think Mom and Dad are?" Jessie whispered so Timmy wouldn't hear.

"There!" I pointed. A gang of Returners in silver suits dragged Mom and Dad out of the RV and through the crowd to the circle of torches. Their hands were tied, and they were gagged.

"What are they going to do to them?" I squeaked, my throat twisted in a hideous panic.

"Nothing, if I can help it! That's Serena Blake!" Jessie pointed at a girl with short black hair. "She's not messing with *my* family." She surged forward.

"Wait!" Eddie grabbed her arm. "There's too many of them." More and more Returners were joining the gathering, forming new, bigger circles, until a vast crowd surrounded the hilltop.

"We have to do something," Jessie said.

"We should give them what they want," Gordon said.

"What's that?" Jessie asked

"Dan," Gordon said. "He's the alien."

"He isn't an alien," Jessie said.

"He *is*," Gordon said. "He wants to go back to Kepler 22b."

"Shut up, Gordon! Just shut up!" I shoved him in the chest and he fell backward. "Don't say another word."

The whole Kepler 22b thing seemed totally stupid and embarrassing now. I didn't want to go there anymore. I wasn't a wack job like the Returners, and I wasn't an alien, either. I wanted to stay here on Earth with my family and my friends, Eddie and . . .

Gordon looked up at me. His eyes swam with tears.

"I'm sorry," he said. "I thought you wanted to go back to your family on Kepler 22b."

"I've changed my mind, okay?"

Gordon's shoulders heaved, and big tears rolled down his cheeks.

And suddenly I realized he'd been telling the truth. Eddie hadn't believed I was an alien. He'd just come along for laughs. But Gordon had taken me seriously. He'd totally believed that I was from Kepler 22b and had done everything possible to help me get back there.

But I wasn't an alien, and the Returners had never been abducted by the superior species. In fact, there was no freakin' superior species. I wasn't even sure Kepler 22b existed. My crazy mission had put Mom and Dad in danger, and I had just been really mean to my second-best friend, who was only trying to help me. Gordon was stuck on the ground like a beetle on his back.

I was the most horrible kid on Earth. No wonder I didn't have many friends.

Returners were still arriving. Nothing else was happening.

"Don't be ridiculous. You aren't an alien," Jessie said. "I was there when you were born. In Mom and Dad's bedroom. Mom had you in the middle of the night. You might be weird, but you're definitely human."

"You *said* I was an alien. At breakfast that day." My

voice sounded like it belonged to someone else. "And there are no photos of me as a baby in Mom's album."

"Yeah, I know," Jessie said. "Her camera was broken when you were born. I know because I broke it. And she didn't get a new one for ages. I was just messing with you."

"And I found a newspaper clipping about a meteor. Something came to Earth from outer space on the day I was born."

"Oh yeah? Coincidence. It wasn't you. You're definitely a Kendal. You have the Kendal tombstone tooth, don't you?" She pulled down her lower lip. One tooth on the bottom row stuck out in front of the others.

I pulled down my lower lip and rubbed my fingers over my teeth.

"That's heredity," Jessie said. "Genetics. DNA. You're my brother. A Kendal. A human. Weird, but human."

I nodded and turned away. I felt like my tear ducts might start leaking. Jessie was my sister. Timmy was my brother. And Mom and Dad were . . . in danger!

"We have to save them," I said. "I'm going to give myself up."

"No way. I'm the oldest, and right now I'm responsible for all of you," Jessie said.

"It isn't Dan they want, anyway," Eddie said. "They want an alien spaceship. They're looking for one now." He pointed to the searchlight in the sky.

Eddie might be a potato-chip addict, but today he was a genius as well.

"Great!" Jessie said. "Where are we going to get one of those on a Wednesday night?"

"I might be able to help you with that." Gordon rocked himself from side to side as he tried to get up.

I held out my hand to help him.

As you know, Gordon doesn't do touching. But this time he grabbed my hand and hauled himself upright.

"Sorry, Gordon. Sorry I pushed you. Sorry for everything," I said.

"Thanks, Dan," he said, and he shook my hand

politely. When he let go, he didn't reach for his disinfectant spray.

I didn't know why he stuck by me when I was such a useless friend. I hadn't even written a message by his picture on the Wall of Wonders at school. I could have written *Genius!!!* or something. But his photo came down without a single comment.

Gordon had supplied the Cryogenics Practitioner's Secret Ingredient.

Gordon had suggested the candy-store moneymaking scheme.

Gordon had built the Supreme Communications Device.

And now Gordon was offering to supply an alien spacecraft to distract the Returners. He was a genius and a true friend.

"What do you need?" I asked.

# 29

## The Alien Mother Ship

"I need a camera, a laptop, a projector, and something that looks like an alien spaceship," Gordon said.

"Get real!" Jessie said.

But she didn't know Gordon the Geek the way Eddie and I did.

"You have the laptop, right?" I said.

Gordon nodded.

"Can we use the camera on your phone?" I asked Jessie.

She thrust the phone into Gordon's hand. "Try not to break it."

Gordon selected the thin-crust laptop from the collection in his briefcase and pulled out miles of cable. No wonder he'd bent the luggage rack on my bike. He was carrying a complete set of IT-specialist's gear.

"What's the plan, Gordon?" I asked.

"If I connect the camera and the laptop and then run

a cable into the back of the searchlight," Gordon said calmly, "I hope to be able to project the image of a spacecraft into the sky. We just have to take a picture of something that looks kind of like a spaceship."

Timmy held up his Duplo model. "Vroom, vroom," he said.

"Timmy, you're a genius too," I said. "If you make a spaceship, Gordon can do a magic trick with it."

Eddie and I left Gordon in charge of the techie stuff while Jessie and Timmy built an alien spaceship out of Duplo bricks for him to photograph.

The searchlight was a huge industrial-size thing that the Returners had transported here by hitching it to the back of a van. It was mounted on a tripod and operated by a crew member from *Star Trek*. He sat holding the two huge handles and swept the beam of light across the sky and back again. Every time he changed direction, the crowd hummed expectantly, but there was no spaceship in the sky and they were getting restless. We didn't have much time.

A ladder with a zillion steps led to the top of the tripod.

"We have to get that guy down," Eddie said.

Eddie knew how I felt about ladders, so he chose my moment of weakness to needle me.

"I don't know why you thought you were an alien in the first place," he said.

"It seemed like a good idea at the time," I said.

"And now?"

I shrugged.

Eddie raised his solidarity eyebrows and patted me on the back.

"How are we going to get rid of Mr. Star Trek?" he asked.

I had the answer, and it didn't involve a ladder. "It's okay—he's wearing a red shirt. He'll do as he's told," I said. I'd seen every episode of *Star Trek* ever made and all the movies. The characters in the red shirts were from Engineering. They never argued with the captain.

"Excuse me!" I shouted up.

The guy ignored me.

"Hey, Trekkie!"

He peered down.

"Captain Kirk wants you on the bridge!"

The man nodded, climbed down the ladder, and disappeared into the crowd.

Eddie climbed the ladder, all eight steps of it, the cable in his hand.

"You ready, Gordon?" I called over to the Geek.

168

He gave a thumbs-up, and Eddie inserted the plug into the socket.

The searchlight went off for a second. When it came on again, the Duplo model hovered directly over the playground.

"Vroom, vroom!" my little brother shouted in delight.

The Returners went crazy. The crowd surged forward as one.

The flaming torches had gone out, but even flames would not have stopped them. Every single Returner wanted to be on that Duplo spacecraft. They moved toward the playground, directly below Gordon's projection —the playground, where Mom and Dad were tied up.

"Mom and Dad are going to be crushed!" Jessie screamed.

"Mommy! Daddy!" Timmy yelled, and burst into tears.

"Move the spaceship!" I shouted up to Eddie. But he couldn't hear me over the cries of the nutjob Returners.

It didn't matter that they weren't perfect parents. They were the only parents I had, and I didn't want them to be crushed to death. Eddie didn't realize the danger they were in. I had to move that searchlight.

Eight steps is a lot when you don't like heights.

I gripped the handrails and put my foot on the first step. There was chaos all around me—people screaming, tripping over each other as they rushed to reach the alien spaceship—but I had to concentrate.

Second step. Third step. I moved quickly before my brain could register what I was doing. I didn't look at the ground. I kept my eyes focused on the ladder rungs right in front of my nose. My feet did the work of pushing me upward. I did the rest, keeping my brain from telling me to be afraid.

The alien spaceship wasn't real. We'd put it there. It was an illusion. A bit like the danger of climbing an eight-step ladder. I couldn't die from falling off this tripod. No

170

one was going to Kepler 22b on that Duplo spaceship. But Mom and Dad could die if those nutters trampled all over them.

Seventh step. Eighth step and I'd done it. I hauled myself up beside Eddie, grabbed the searchlight, and swung it away.

As the Duplo spaceship moved across the sky, a cry of panic rose from the crowd. They must have thought it was leaving without them. Every single Returner on Park Hill Fields broke ranks and stumbled down the hill, following the fake spacecraft.

"Leave it hanging over the school," Eddie said. "Who knows, they might have to cancel classes tomorrow if the building is occupied."

"Let's get Mom and Dad," I said.

Eddie scrambled off the ladder first. The ground shimmered as I looked down, but I wasn't going to let a little bit of vertigo get in my way now. I jumped after him and ran to my human parents.

I ripped the gag away from Mom's mouth. "Daniel!" she croaked as I fumbled to undo the industrial-size cable ties at her wrists.

"Careful," Eddie said. "Those are police-issue restraints. You might tighten them accidentally. I'll show you how to

release them. You okay, Mr. Kendal?" He helped Dad to his feet.

I led Mom away from the rendezvous point.

"Mommy!" Timmy yelled, and grabbed her around the knees. She lifted her handcuffed hands over his head and hugged him close.

"Hello, sweetheart," she croaked, and buried her face in his hair.

Dad joined us. "Well done, kids," he said. "But will someone tell me what's going on?"

"I think it was a case of mistaken identity," I said, and hugged my average-height, balding, totally human dad.

# 30

## The Trouble with the Police

It took us ages to get home. I suggested that Mom and Dad ride the bikes so they could get home quickly, but every time Mom tried to say goodbye, she grabbed the nearest child and sobbed into her or his hair. Or, in my case, chest. She couldn't reach the top of my head.

"I think it would be prudent to stick together," Gordon said, edging away from my overwrought mother to avoid being hugged and cried on.

"I agree," Dad said. "We thought we might be separated forever. I want all of you where I can see you." He grabbed Jessie by the shoulders and me by the waist and pulled us in for a group hug.

Then we started home. Eddie buzzed around us on his mini motorbike. Mom pushed her bike along, with Timmy in his child seat, and I pushed mine. Gordon trailed behind.

Police sirens wailed on the other side of town, over toward our school.

"Sounds like the whole police force is out," Dad said.

"I guess we'll have to tell them we were kidnapped," Mom said wearily.

"If you do that, you'll have to go down to the station," Eddie said.

"They might not believe you," Gordon added. "You could be arrested and locked up in the same cell as your kidnappers."

"I don't want that!" Mom wailed. "I just want to get home safely and lock the door and forget that all this happened."

Dad didn't say anything, but his deep worry lines were back.

I tried to send him a telepathic message: *Don't call the police. Don't call the police.* I hoped Gordon and Eddie were sending it too. Best-friend telepathy was working, and this time we were all thinking the same thing. We didn't want to explain ourselves to the police.

When we turned the corner onto Beechwood Road, a police car was already parked outside our house.

My stomach lurched. It wasn't vertigo this time, it was police-ophobia. I'd caught it from Eddie.

"I'm off." Eddie revved up his shady motorbike. "Will you be all right now, Mr. Kendal?"

"Sure, Ed. Thanks for your help." Dad slapped him on the back.

"I'll head home as well," Gordon said.

"Do you think you can convert my bike to methane?" Eddie asked Gordon as they turned to leave. "Farts are methane, right?"

"Of course," Gordon said. "Methane is a form of natural gas. It is possible to convert a gasoline combustion engine to run off natural gas."

"Great."

"See you tomorrow," I called after them. "If I'm not under arrest."

Just before Eddie turned the corner, I heard a sound. It might have been the motorbike backfiring, but on the other hand, it probably wasn't.

A police officer climbed out of the police car as we reached the house. I felt as if I'd just entered the chasm of doom. Everything I'd done during the day had been illegal one way or another.

"Did you report the theft of a satellite dish?" the police officer asked Dad.

"I did, but it's back now." Dad pointed to the dish on the front wall.

"Wasting police time is a very serious matter," the police officer said. "Are you sure you're the owner of this house? I was expecting someone Japanese." The police officer pointed to our stupid house name, Konnichiwa.

"I thought it was more interesting than calling the house 'Hello.'" Dad looked embarrassed, but I don't think the police officer noticed.

"Has your satellite dish been stolen or not?"

"No, sorry," Dad said. "I was mistaken."

The police officer took out his notebook and looked us over suspiciously.

"Something highly suspect is going on. The school has been taken over for some kind of unauthorized festival. You aren't part of that, are you?"

Dad might be unwilling to discuss how I came to be born, but he'd never lie to the police. I had to speak for him.

"We were at the park," I said. "For a family picnic."

The police officer eyed us up and down.

"Where's your picnic basket?" he said. "And your blanket?"

"Some crazies dressed as *Star Trek* characters stole them," I said.

The police officer nodded wisely.

"Well, I'd better go see what they're up to." He put his notebook away. "Should I consider the case of the missing satellite dish closed?"

"Yes, please," Dad said. "Sorry to waste your time, officer."

"Good night." The police officer nodded curtly and left.

"Thanks, Bean," Dad said when he'd gone. "I thought we were going to be arrested."

"Would you mind calling me Dan from now on?"

"Of course, Dan." Dad reached up and patted me on the shoulder.

"Hope he arrests Serena Blake. Then I can have her part in the school play," Jessie said.

"Let's go inside," Mom said. "No wonder the police officer thought we were part of that mob. Just look at us! Timmy out in public in his pajamas, Jessie's hair in a haystack, and your jeans halfway up your legs, Bean— I mean Dan. You've grown again. We'll go on a special mother-and-son shopping trip next weekend."

"You aren't going shopping without me," Jessie said.

Mom looked at me, one solidarity eyebrow raised. The Kendal-family telepathy was working overtime. I knew exactly what she was thinking.

"Sure," I said. "Let's make it a family trip."

Jessie raised her hand up for a high-five. I slapped it playfully away.

Mom and Dad exchanged one of their telepathically charged looks and smiled.

"Come on, Timmy, time for bed," Mom said. "I was thinking, Dan . . . would you mind switching rooms with Timmy? There'd be more room for his train set and Duplo bricks in the room you have now. We could get a loft bed for the smaller room."

"Cool!" I said. "Can I have my own laptop? I know where we can get a really good deal."

"Not fair! If he's getting a computer, I'm getting a computer," Jessie said.

"We'll talk about it in the morning," Dad said. "Right now all I want is a cup of coffee." He ushered us into the house and shut the door, leaving the crazy world of Returners and aliens outside.

# 31
## The True Meaning of Friendship

"Does your dad have any more of those laptops?" I asked
Eddie the next day at school.

"I think so. But you won't need a laptop on Kepler
22b," Eddie said.

"Different voltage," Gordon said.

"The Kepler 22b mission is officially over," I said.

"Thank goodness for that. Daniel Kendal has landed." Eddie stuffed a fistful of potato chips into his mouth.

"Glad you're staying," Gordon said without looking up from his laptop screen.

I'm so lucky. I have the two best friends on Earth.

If there were alien kids on Kepler 22b, they were going to have to do without me. I'd be staying right here. We humans have to stick together.